Inspired by her 14-year-old daughter's *Breakfast Club* T-shirt, first time author, Julie Ives, woke up one morning finding herself putting pencil to paper, furiously writing down the story of *Welcome to Welby Island* that was gaining steam in her head. She could imagine the characters and the setting but needed to bring them to life through the written word. She doesn't equate herself to any one character but hints that there just may be a little of her in each of them.

Julie was born in New Jersey, attended high school in Huntington NY, and went onto college in Connecticut, where she met her husband Howie and married in 1993. However, the sandy beaches of the Sunshine State called to them in 2000, where they live with their daughter, Maggie.

I dedicate this book to my daughter, Maggie. She is and always will be my inspiration.

Julie Ives

WELCOME TO WELBY ISLAND

AUSTIN MACAULEY PUBLISHERS™

LONDON • CAMBRIDGE • NEW YORK • SHARJAH

Copyright © Julie Ives (2018)

Ordering Information:
Quantity sales: special discounts are available on quantity purchases by corporations, associations, and others. For details, contact the publisher at the address below.

Publisher's Cataloging-in-Publication data
Ives, Julie
Welcome to Welby Island

ISBN 9781641824613 (Paperback)
ISBN 9781641824620 (Hardback)
ISBN 9781641824637 (E-Book)

The main category of the book — FICTION / Romance / General

www.austinmacauley.com/us

First Published (2018)
Austin Macauley Publishers LLC
40 Wall Street, 28th Floor
New York, NY 10005
USA

mail-usa@austinmacauley.com
+1 (646) 5125767

I would like to thank my dear friends Karen, Lisa, Tricia, and Tracey for taking the time to read my original manuscript; flaws and all. Your honest critiques and words of encouragement gave me the confidence to continue forward and not give up.

And to my PP (Pen Pal) Carol, thank you for responding to my email. I know you weren't interviewing for new friends, but I took a leap of faith, and I'm sorry to tell you, but you have a new friend. Thank you for everything.

Every once in a while, there are bumps in the road called life. Every bump in the road can make us stronger. Every bump in the road can alter our course. Here is a story about five people, from different walks of life, who were brought together because of the bumps in the road they encountered. The journey they will go on together will make them stronger, make them love harder, and will help them to continue down the road called 'life'. That is, if they are able to follow the road to enlightenment, which has taken them to Welby Island, off the coast of Washington State, and put them in the hands of world renowned life coaches: Micah and Blair Claine. They come to the island as strangers, but through anger, humor, sweat, and tears, they will leave the island forever bonded.

Meet Leanne, Devon, Amber, Leonard, and Rosalie, and follow them on their journey:

Leanne Dougherty
35-year-old mother of twins, Luke and Lindsey; married to Blake.

Devon Davis
32-year-old British Rock star; single.

Amber Quinn
21-year-old model/actress; single at the moment.

Leonard Mathers
25-year-old computer geek; always single.

Rosalie Grant
40-year-old. Top Dollar real estate agent; divorced.

Micah Claine
48-year-old life coach; married to Blair.

Blair Claine
46-year-old life coach; married to Micah.

Chapter 1
Leanne Dougherty

"Oh for God's sake, Blake, why are you making such a big deal out of this? Yes, I drank a couple of glasses of wine last night and, yes, I fell asleep in the chaise lounge on the deck at ten o'clock at night. And do you want to know why?" said Leanne.

Blake folded his newspaper and pushed his empty coffee cup aside, and replied, "I could say no, but I'm sure you will tell me anyway."

Leanne looked at his smug face and continued, "I was out there lying under the stars, trying to figure out why I am so miserably exhausted and unhappy."

Blake snickered and said, "What is it that actually exhausts you and makes you unhappy, Leanne? I give you everything you need or want. You don't work and you haven't volunteered with a charity in over a year."

Leanne revved up her engines and took off from the station, "If you were ever home to actually see or listen to what my days are like, you would be head first into a bottle of hundred-year-old whiskey that you are so fond of. You have no idea what my day entails…first getting the twins out of bed for school is like trying to revive an ant with mouth to mouth for Christ's sake, then when they do rise, they turn into snails. It takes them forever to get from the bed to the breakfast table."

Leanne, the Locomotive, is full steam ahead. No stopping her now.

Feeling frustrated, Blake countered, "Leanne, they are six-year-old, first graders. They have no comprehension of urgency. Maybe you should…"

Leanne shot him daggers with her eyes and said, "Oh there it is! Maybe you should Leanne and maybe you could Leanne. Why don't you Blake stay home one morning, no…no, not just one morning, a whole day, and walk in my shoes. How about that, Blake? Wake them, feed them, pack their lunches, only to be told they will not eat the carrots that you just peeled and then precisely cut into little circles, just how they like them. Oh, and then get them dressed; that's a circus in its self, but after you somehow succeed, corral them into the car. 'Oh, wait Daddy, I forgot my rock for show and tell', or 'Daddy, I don't want to go to school. Annie Butler is really, really mean to me', and then once you do get them to school; spending 40 minutes in the car line, only to be stopped by Penny Perkins, PTA Queen Bee, and be told that you just have to meet her for coffee to discuss the upcoming fundraiser, even though you are in the t-shirt you slept in, no bra, and a pair of old grungy sweats and slippers, you do it. Want to know why? Because she is Penny Fucking Perkins, and no one says no to her!"

"Leanne, listen, I know your mornings are crazy..." Blake began, only to be cut off again by a raging mad Leanne.

"My mornings, oh, that is just the beginning. After I escape Penny Fucking Perkins, I, then, stop to pick up your dry cleaning that I forgot the day before, which if you remember, made you a 'tad bit crazy' because you wouldn't have your lucky golf shirt for 36 holes of golf with your important client today. Lordy, you don't know how the guilt ate me up on that one!" Leanne bellowed.

With his anger rising, Blake replied, "Leanne, don't go there. You know me being a partner at Jacoby and Tanner requires me to schmooze my clients and..."

"Oh yeah, you schmooze them and booze them, and spend hours lingering over Chateau Briand and four-hundred-dollar bottles of wine, five days a week! When Blake, tell me, when was the last time we sat down for dinner as a family, or better yet, when was the last time you came to one of Luke's soccer games or Lindsey's dance recitals, huh, or tucked them into bed, when Blake?"

Leanne, the Locomotive, was running out of steam and now drowning in tears.

Blake stood up, sighed, and said, "Leanne, I know you do a lot of running around during the day. I have told you numerous times to hire a nanny, and every time, you refuse. If you are too exhausted, as you say, to take care of our kids, then I will hire someone that can."

Through tear blurred eyes she looked at him, stood up to leave the room and as she did, she turned to him, and said, "Blake...fuck you."

Leanne, the Locomotive, had derailed.

Chapter 2
Devon Davis

"What the bloody hell?" Devon grabbed the pillow to ward off the shot of blinding sunlight that invaded his bedroom.

"Rise and shine, Rock Star. We need to talk," Devon's manager, Gordy Little, was not in a good mood.

"What time is it? I can't open my eyes, nonetheless carry out a conversation before noon," mumbled Devon from beneath the pillow.

Gordy picked up a shirt off the floor, threw it at Devon, and said, "Devon, get up, put some damn clothes on, and meet me in the kitchen."

Devon rolled over and put the pillow back over his head. However, knowing that Gordy would be back to torment his throbbing head, he slowly rolled out of bed with one eye open and headed for the loo.

***

"Okay, Gordy. This bloody well better be important. I had a late night and don't manage well on a few hours of sleep," Devon said as he inhaled his coffee.

"Well, Devon, that is what I am here to talk to you about. How much of last night do you remember?" asked Gordy.

"Huh?" Devon rubbed his face hoping to wake up his brain, "Let's see, we closed our last set at midnight; a huge success if I do say so myself. Hit the bus at 12:30 a.m., stopped off at Winkles for a celebratory cocktail or two, which ended up as a crazy late night rave and from there it gets a little fuzzy…what's this all about, Gordy?"

"Well, let me pull the fuzz out of your brain through your ass," said a not so happy Gordy. "Last night, after your so called crazy night rave, you were seen leaving the bar with a beautiful brunette by the name of Kelsey. Do you remember Kelsey, Devon?"

Devon put his face in his hands and replied, "Vaguely."

Gordy sat forward and said, "Well, let me make it less vague for you. Kelsey is a fan, a groupie, a part of the wolf pack that follows you to every concert, but tonight you happen to be playing here, at home, in L.A. So she actually followed you to Winkles, where you proceeded to order her drinks, flirt her up, and asked her if she would, and I quote this, 'Like to go play romper room'. You were very persuasive and got as far as your front door with Kelsey in tow, which is when her friend that she left at the bar and Jake showed up, and had to drag her out of there."

Devon sipped his coffee and sighed, "Okay, so her friend freaked out. Jake, the savior, once again rode in on his white horse to save the non-protesting, non-in-distress damsel. Seriously, Gordy, this is why you woke me?"

"No," Gordy said, "The reason I woke you is that the non-protesting, non-in-distress damsel, Kelsey, is 16 years old and just happens to be the daughter of the L.A. police chief, who would very much like a command performance from you in his office in one hour. So, shower and get dressed, Romeo."

"Oh, bloody hell."

Devon stood, staggered, and left the room.

Chapter 3
Amber Quinn

Click, click, click the sound of the camera startled Amber back into reality. She was running late for her appointment with Giovanni, her photographer. As she was about to enter his loft, someone stepped in front of her, and started wildly snapping pictures. Since her modeling jobs had dwindled down to shampoo commercials, and her aspirations of acting needed some tweaking, she thought that maybe this was an adoring fan.

Amber took off her sunglasses and in her sugary southern voice, said, "Well, aren't you just the sweetest. Would you like an autograph, too?"

The handsome young man said, "No thanks, the pictures are all I need."

He turned and walked away.

Hmm, Amber thought, *well, okie dokie.*

Once inside, she headed straight to hair and make-up.

* * *

The next morning, at the ungodly hour of nine a.m., Amber's cell phone was vibrating like a lonely woman's 'helping hand'.

"Hellooo," was all she could manage. Amber had been out at the night club until the late hours of the morning and could hardly open her baby blues.

"Amber, Amber, is that you, beautiful? You need to get your perky little country girl tatas down to the loft pronto! Giovanni is on a rampage. I cannot understand a word he is saying. He's ranting in Italian and we all know that cannot be good," Seth, Giovanni's assistant, was shouting into the phone.

"Okay, Okay, umm...give me a half hour."

Amber jumped out of bed, took one look in the mirror, and said, "Oh dang."

She dressed, grabbed her knock-off Coach bag, sunglasses, and rushed out the door.

* * *

Giovanni was pacing and swearing in three languages when Amber arrived. "Gio," she said, "What in the world is going on? Seth woke me out of a sound sleep and said to get here as fast as I can?"

"Ah Bella, my sweet Bella, come, come sit." Giovanni had never looked this crazed, so she sat. Giovanni picked up an envelope from the table and said, "My Bella, I have something to show you. Now please trust me when I say, umm, this is not good. No, not good, my Bella."

Amber grabbed the envelope, opened it, and out slid a dozen pictures of a girl she had never seen before. She looked at Giovanni and asked, "Who is this?"

Giovanni took her hands in his and replied, "Ah, my Bella, that is you, and now these, these horrible pictures of a skinny, sunken eyed, hallow cheeked girl, with no hope of modeling or acting ever, ever again, are all over the internet. My Bella, my Bella, I think it is time as they say in the movies, to click your heels together and head back to Kansas, Dorothy, no?"

Chapter 4
Leaonard Mathers

"Hey, Leonard, wait up a minute. Hey, how you doing, man? Long time no talk, how's everything?" The yapping Chihuahua was the annoying Frank, or as he liked to be called 'Frankie Baby'. Frankie Baby was the head of Human Resources at the most elite computer software company on the West Coast; Statistic Analog REM Technology, known as S.A.R.T Inc., which unfortunately for Leonard, was created and run by his mega rich, mega brilliant, mega busy parents; John and Ellen Mathers. Leonard is the only human creation they ever made or, otherwise, referred to as their only child. Again, unfortunately for Leonard, he inherited their brilliance and is known around S.A.R.T's lab as 'boy prodigy'.

Frankie Baby put his hand on Leonard's shoulder and said, "So, Lenny, I hear you got a little side poker game going on in the basement, and I want in."

Leonard kept walking and replied, "I have no idea what you are talking about."

"Come on, Len. It's me, Frankie. You know I can keep it on the QT; that is, of course, I'm dealt in," said Frankie Baby.

Leonard stopped in his tracks. He was sweating profusely and his thick black bottle lens glasses kept sliding down his nose. He turned to Frank and said, "You swear you won't tell a soul. Swear to me, Frank. You will keep it under wraps?"

"Yeah, yeah, Lenny. You got it, my lips are zipped. So when, where, and how much is the pot?" Frankie Baby was beaming. He had heard about this game for months and now he was in.

Leonard gave him the details and hurried into the lab. He knew he had just made a huge mistake, but what was done was done.

***

Friday, at midnight, was the date and the time, the place, the basement of S.A.R.T; the belly of his parent's love child. Leonard was pretty darn proud of his underground casino. Ever since being banned from Vegas, he had to come up with some other way to get his fix. It's not that he needed the money; truth be told, he got booted from Vegas because he always won. Word on the strip was, he was fixing the tables, but nobody could explain how, so they banned him. Leonard didn't mind. He always found Vegas a little over whelming, but oh how he missed the cha-ching of the slots and the clack of the dice, so he knew he had to create his own 'oases' and that he did. He always meant to keep it to himself, but once a few of his co-workers caught wind of the belly of the basement casino; things steam rolled forward. He thought about charging an entrance fee, but then that would put the 'ill' in 'legal'.

Friday night started out as usual; a few co-workers came by to hit the slots, which he originally filled with his Vegas winnings, but since no one has hit the jackpot, the money kept going in rather than going out. Others came for the roulette table, which was 'manned', so to speak, by what Leonard considered one of his greatest creations; a Robot named James, and of course, the midnight poker game. It was 11:55 p.m. and Leonard was dreading the arrival of Frankie Baby, and two seconds later, he knew why. Frank entered the room with a dozen little old ladies quacking like ducks, approached Leonard, and asked, "Leonard, my man, how's it rolling?"

Frankie was in rare form, or ninety-proof, probably both.

"What the heck, Frank! Who are all of these old ladies?" Immediately after the words left his lips, Leonard regretted it.

Out of nowhere, the purple hair one wacked him upside his head and said, "Who you calling old, sonny?"

Rubbing his head, Leonard grabbed Frankie by his arm, and pulled him aside, "Frank, you promised not to tell a soul!"

"I know, but my Granny overheard me talking to my wife and then she called her bunko club and well, here they are. They want to play bingo," said Frank.

"We don't have bingo for grannies here, Frank!" Leonard screamed.

The room went dead silent. A mass of white, blue, and purple hair descended upon Leonard, swatting at him with their oversized, money filled granny purses. Things went from bad to worse when 'Frankie Baby' lit a cigar and the fire alarm blared, which in turn set off the state of the art sprinkler system.

All Leonard could think, as the firemen bursted through the door, was, *I gambled and I lost.*

Chapter 5
Rosalie Grant

"Absolutely, I can show you the house at 6924 Canyon Drive. Let's say two o'clock, shall we? Perfect, see you then," Rosalie hung up with the potential client. She was beside herself with anticipation. It had been almost a year since she had a listing of this magnitude. She had been so excited and in such a hurry, three months ago, to sign the contract for the listing of Emerald Estate; a magnificent mansion on the cliff in LaSalla, with a breathtaking view of the Pacific. The estate encompassed four acres of prime real estate and she knew it would list for at least seven million dollars; however, what she did not anticipate was catching her six-hundred-dollar, four inch spiked, Tommy Woo heel, in a crack of the cobblestone walkway. She went down like a redwood in the forest. To break her fall, she twisted her body left in search of the plush green lawn, instead she ended up on a statue of the Virgin Mary with her praying hands; sharply snapping Rosalie's left femur in two. If the irony of it wasn't painful enough, the pain in her leg that still lingered after the fall, was.

Rubbing her leg she thought, *I guess it would be okay to take another Oxy*, even though she had popped one an hour ago. The way she looked at it, it was all for the client and the huge commission from the sale of Emerald Estate would bring her.

* * *

By noon, Rosalie was pacing the floor. When her ex-husband, Harold; a.k.a, her pill supplier, dropped by unexpectedly. She was elated to see him. Rosalie answered the door and threw her arms around Harold, and gave him a big fat kiss on the lips.

"Whoa, whoa. Easy, girl," said Harold.

"You are just the person I wanted to see," Rosalie bellowed. Harold knew exactly why she was so happy to see him, but that would be short lived once she found out why he was there.

"And why is that Rosalie?" Harold teased as he entered the large foyer of the huge house that Rosalie just had to have and which he paid for.

Rosalie reached into the pocket of her Stephan Wang silk wrap dress and produced an empty pill bottle. "Well, lookie here. It's empty," she said in her best little girl voice; a game they had played since he delivered her first not so 'legit' pain pills after she broke her leg and her orthopedic surgeon would not renew her 30 day supply.

Harold cleared his throat and bravely said, "Well, actually, that is why I am here, Rosalie. I think it's time you got off the pills…"

"Harold!" she screamed. All traces of the sweet little girl voice were gone, "You are going to get me more pills right this minute! Do you hear me? Do you see me? I'm in pain!"

"Well, actually, Rosalie, you look fine to me. A little high strung, maybe, but in pain, no. Sorry, Rosie. I've got to cut off your supply, and my professional opinion is for you to get some physical therapy for your leg," he said with such authority he had to look around to see if someone else had said it.

Harold took one look at Rosalie and saw the bull was ready to gore the matador, so he turned, and ran for the front door. Rosalie was screaming all kinds of profanity at him but he didn't break his stride. He flung open the door and just about made it down the front steps when a four inch spiked heel nailed him in the head. He made it to his Beemer, jumped in, and put it in reverse. He could hear Rosalie yelling, "'In your professional opinion', that's a load of crap. You're a fucking chiropractor!"

Needless to say, Rosalie did not make the two o'clock showing.

Chapter 6
And, so It Begins

Leanne arrived at SoCal Executive Airport, via taxi, an hour before the scheduled 'Meet and Greet' with Micah and Blair Claine of the so-called world renowned Claine Enlightenment Retreat. It wasn't that she was overly anxious to head down the road to enlightenment. However, if she didn't do something to help her figure out why her world was collapsing around her, she would continue to walk through life in a funk. When she entered the airport, it was empty, which oddly enough, she found comforting, because, in reality, she really didn't like people. That was a concern to her because the old Leanne would be the first to organize a get together with friends, step up to help with any charity, and was the shoulder to lean on for any and all that came to her with their woes. Resigned, she flopped down onto a cracked, mustard-colored chair, reached into her handbag for one of the two personal items they were allowed to bring. Leanne chose a photo of the twins, and the *Sixty Sides of Gray* trilogy, which in hindsight, may not have been such a smart choice, if what she heard about the book was true.

***

Devon Davis despised airports. He always felt like he was on display like a store mannequin. He stepped out of the limo, put on his Ray Bans, and grabbed his duffel bag from the driver. Once he got a look at the tin shack called an airport, he relaxed a bit. Seeing only one other person in the room, he snickered and said to himself, *no chance of a mob scene here.*

Considering he was early, and his seating choices were vast, he opted for the corner chair, and proceeded to shake out his newspaper; properly lay it over his face and dozed off.

* * *

"Seth, honestly, I don't know why Gio couldn't have driven me to the airport himself. This was all his idea to save my career," Amber whined.

"Oh, you know Giovanni. He wears his emotions on his sleeve. He would be no good to you," sighed Seth as he parked the Range Rover in front of the small metal building.

"Huh?" both Amber and Seth said at the same time.

"This can't be right," Amber said, "How are those big, ole planes going to take off from that itty bitty runway?"

Seth hopped out of the Rover and opened the back hatch to retrieve Amber's bright pink suitcase, all the while trying to coax Amber out of the front seat.

"Come on, sweet cheeks. Let's shake a leg," he chirped. Reluctantly, Amber exited the vehicle. Seth grabbed her wrist and dragged her along like another piece of luggage. "Let's move it, Pumpkin Bumpkin. You don't want to miss your flight to the unknown," said Seth as he opened the door to the small room.

Once inside, Amber turned to Seth and squeaked, "I think we made a wrong turn. This can't be right. Where are all the people and the big airplanes?"

Seth looked around. Sitting on opposite sides of the room were two people, he cleared his throat and said, "Um, excuse me, but is this the waiting area for the flight to the 'wherever' retreat?"

Neither of the two occupants answered, just nodded without looking up.

"Oh goodie, here you go, Doll Face. Have a nice flight."

And on that note, Seth dropped the luggage and made a bee line out the door; leaving a wide eyed, open mouthed Amber in his wake.

Amber could not move. Finally, from the corner of the room, the man said, "Take a seat, Barbie. It's going to be a while."

* * *

"Now, Leonard, you know your mother and I feel this is the best option for you. Running an illegal casino in the basement of our multi-million dollar company was not using your God given brain. However, three months at the Claine Enlightenment Retreat should give you plenty of time to think and reflect on the error of your ways."

John Mathers was not a force to be reckoned with. And Ellen Mathers was, well, just not a force of any kind. She actually looked like a bobble head; the kind you see in a hula skirt on the dash board of the young surfer dude's jeep. Anytime John spoke, Ellen bobbled.

"I know, Dad, but seriously, could you not just give me some credit here. I created state of the art slot machines with computers not even thought of yet. Seriously, did you see the robot Roulette dealer? He rocked. If you would just listen to me, I bet we could take those prototypes, tweak them a bit, and make a killing."

"Sorry, son. Your betting days are behind you," his father said as they pulled into the parking lot of the two by four, metal shack called SoCal Executive Airport.

* * *

Rosalie pulled into the gravel parking lot of SoCal Executive Airport and cursed under her breath as the clink of gravel hit the sides of her hundred-thousand-dollar Stallion TLX 240. She parked her car outside the front door of the tin can of an airport and got out, careful not to trip on her four inch Harvey Benton pumps. Rosalie marched inside demanding to know where the valet was as the four other people in the room stared at her blankly. Rosalie smoothed her three-hundred-dollar Rina Colbert skirt and asked again, "Can someone please tell me where the parking valet is?"

Silence filled the room.

"Hello, are you all deaf? I asked, where is the parking valet?"

Well, that did it. The room exploded with laughter.

Then, thankfully, the woman in jeans and a white T-shirt approached her and said, "You wouldn't happen to be here for the flight to enlightenment, would you?"

Miffed, Rosalie replied, "I don't believe that is any of your business."

The woman, who looked like she just tumbled out of a cloth dryer, replied, "Well, if you are, I am sorry to inform you but there is no fucking parking valet, and there is no fucking concierge."

Leanne, the Locomotive, was back on the rails.

Just as Rosalie was ready to turn on her four inch heels and huff away, a stocky man with a snowcap of white hair walked in and said, "Howdy, ya'll? My name is Chet, and I am going to be your pilot today. We should be ready for departure in approximately ten minutes, right after I file my flight plan and give the plane a once over."

Rosalie sauntered up to him, smoothing her skirt again, and said, "Excuse me. Chet, is it? Would you happen to know where the parking valet is? You see, I have my car out front and I really need it parked in an environmentally friendly garage. Could you be a dear and see to that?"

Chet rubbed his chin and said, "Well, ma'am, I'm afraid we don't have no valet service here, or any kind of e-viro-mental friendly garage, but here's what I can do for you; see that tarp over yonder, you can park your ve-hi-cle under there. Can't guarantee it will be there when you get back, but you're welcome to it."

Rosalie opened her mouth, thought better of it, and turned on her high heels and exited the building. She pulled her prohibited cellphone out of her purse and dialed.

"Harold, you fucking prick, this is all your fault!" she screamed, "Now get your fat ass out to SoCal executive airport and get my car. Apparently, they don't have valet parking or a fucking parking garage!"

Calming herself before she burst a vein, Rosalie added in a low growl, "And, Harold, if one thing happens to my car while I'm gone, I will twist your scrawny balls off with my bare hands! Do you understand me?"

Harold, being thankful for the distance the phone allotted, said, "Sure. No problem, Rosalie. Have a nice flight."

He hung up pronto.

Once again, Rosalie turned on her four inch heels and went in search of a baggage handler, and then the light bulb went off; if there is no valet, there is no baggage handler. That is when she lost it and screamed, "What the fuck!"

She lugged her bags out of the car and dragged them to the front door. The icing on the cake was when the heel of her left pump snapped like a twig.

Chapter 7

"Okay, ladies and gents, we are ready to board the plane," Chet boomed when he walked in the room. "Grab your luggage and follow me," he directed as he headed out to the tarmac.

Leanne grabbed her carry-on bag and small suitcase, and quickly following after Chet said, "Um, excuse me, Chet. I was wondering…what the hell is that?"

Leanne, the Locomotive, stopped dead on the tracks. The other four practically plowed her over. Amber stared in disbelief at what she was seeing in front of her.

"Well," Chet said, "This here is, Sadie, we have been together for nearly 30 years."

Devon didn't know whether to burst out laughing or belly up to Sadie for a closer look. Rosalie, for once in her life, was speechless.

"Cool," said Leonard, as he quickly moved forward to get a better look.

When Rosalie finally found her voice, she asked, "You don't expect all of us to fit in that thing, nonetheless our luggage."

"Yup," said Chet, "Sadie here will be taking you to Welby Island, off the coast of the fine ole' state of Washington."

Slowly starting to back away, Amber shakily said, "No way am I getting into that teenie, tiny airplane."

"Well," said Chet, "That there is up to you, young lady, but it's the only way to get to Claine Retreat, being that it's on an island and all."

"An island!" all five screeched at once.

"Yup," replied Chet.

Locomotive Leanne started her engine and said, "Wait, wait just a minute. You mean to tell me that we are supposed to climb into that thing and trust you to get us to some island out in the middle of the Pacific Ocean? Where the hell are the Claines? They were supposed to meet us."

"Well, being that it's a six-seater and I have you five, and me to get out to the island, the Claine's told me that they would meet you on the island," Chet explained.

Devon had been analyzing the situation and said, "Let me ask you, Chet. Is there a landing strip on this island?"

"Nope, Sadie here is a sea plane. I set her down in the water, slide her in smooth as silk," replied Chet.

"In the Pacific Ocean?" Rosalie shouted.

"Naw, the Puget Sound. Like I said before, Sadie and I, we've been together a long time, done this a million times. Ya'll come on. I got a schedule to keep. Let's get your luggage loaded," Chet said as he started up the stairs of the plane.

Leonard was right behind him. "Um, Chet, any chance I can sit up front with you?" he asked excitedly.

"Sure, son, somebody's got to," Chet replied.

Reluctantly, the others moved toward the stairs. Leanne climbed up, followed by Devon. Rosalie was struggling with her two huge suitcases when Chet popped his head out the door and said, "Don't think they'll fit; plus, we have a weight limit. You got to choose just one."

Oh boy, oh boy, oh boy, Rosalie looked like someone just told her that she had to go backpacking across the Mojave Desert on a mule.

"What? There is no way I am leaving one of these fifteen-hundred-dollar Vente suitcases behind. All of my belongings are in them!" she said adamantly.

"Well, you can't bring them both," Chet calmly replied.

At this point, Amber was in a catatonic state. She had a terrible fear of flying in big planes, but this sea plane thingy. It will just about be the death of her, figuratively speaking. When she finally found her voice, she squeaked, "Um…Mr. Chet, um, you see, um…I have a fear of flying, so, um, I'm not sure I can get on Sadie."

Chet, seeing that this young girl was pale as a blizzard in Alaska, kindly said, "Little lady, I think you are braver than you know, where you from?"

Chet kept talking, asking Amber questions, as he slowly came down the stairs.

"I live in Los Angeles," she replied meekly.

"Nope, that's not the accent I'm picking up. I'd say you're a country girl, right?" Chet slowly guided Amber toward the plane, talking all the while.

"Um, well, yes, I was born and raised in Sweetwater, Oklahoma. My daddy is a farmer and my momma, she owns the best bakery this side of the Mississippi," Amber replied feeling a little bit more relaxed.

"Well, ain't that fine? I come from a small town right near there. Derby, ever hear of it?" Chet said, as he guided her onto the plane and into the seat next to Devon.

"Well, yes, I have. My Aunt Trudy lives in Derby," Amber said brightly.

Now that Amber was safely seated and buckled in, Chet said, "You see this here good looking fella. He's gonna make sure you have a real nice flight, aren't you, young man?"

Devon was figuring his odds. And out of the three women, he liked his odds. "Yeah, Okay, don't you worry about a thing, Country Girl. You're in good hands," he said with his best rock star grin.

"By the way, Chet, how long is this flight?" asked Leonard, as he loaded and secured Amber's suitcase.

"Sadie here and I can do it in just under three hours," Chet replied, eager to get the show on the road. He turned back to the door and said to Rosalie, "Ma'am, I can arrange that one of your bags is given to whoever picks up your fancy auto-mobile. So, time to make your decision; on or off?"

Rosalie knew she had to get on this plane, but was not happy about leaving one of her Vente bags behind, especially the one with 12 pairs of shoes. "Oh, all right," she huffed. "But if anything happens to that bag, your balls are going to meet the same fate as Harold's," she barked and boarded the plane.

Once everyone was seated, Leanne cleared her throat and said, "Chet, by any chance, would you happen to have any wine on the plane?"

"No, mam. But back there in that there cooler, is some pop and bottled water," Chet said as he strapped in and started the engine.

From behind her, Devon said with humor in his voice, "Well, now we know why you're on the plane to enlightenment; the big 'A' word, I would predict."

Leanne stood up and looked behind her, and shot him her best fuck you look. He just merely smirked.

Locomotive Leanne said, "Well, I guess the big 'A' could also stand for why you're on the plane to enlightenment; for being an Asshole."

Devon stared at her, like he was searching for a witty comeback, but only responded with, "Apparently so."

He turned to the window.

Rosalie popped a tic-tac in her mouth and said, "Well, this should be fun."

Chapter 8

"Okay, folks. As they say on the big jet airliners, buckle up. We will be landing in five, four, three, two, one," said Chet.

Up front, Leonard was hootin' and hollerin' like a teenager. "Oh man, Chet! That was awesome! Landing Sadie smooth like silk, and that you did! Wow, awesome!" Leonard said again.

Chet glided Sadie up to a long wooden dock. Standing at the end of the dock, waving like flags in a hurricane, was a very beautiful couple. The woman had gorgeous, curly, red hair billowing down her back and the blond hunk standing next to her was the stunning replica of Robert Redman, the actor. He smiled brightly and his majestic blue eyes said, "Welcome," in 40 languages.

Rosalie frantically searched through her purse for her compact mirror and lipstick. Devon's tongue was hanging out like a puppy begging to be petted.

Leanne struck as fast as a cobra. "Hey Brit, put your tongue back in your mouth and your…oh my God! Now we know why you're on this plane to enlightenment…you can't keep it in your pants! Great, perfect. Stuck on an island in the middle of nowhere with a perv," she grabbed her bags and headed for the exit.

Rosalie scooted out of her seat and quickly followed on Leanne's heels.

When Devon stood, he looked down and saw Amber clutching the armrest with white knuckles and she had her eyes squeezed tightly shut. He gave her a little nudge and she squealed like a state fair prize winning pig.

Devon sighed and said, "Let's go, Country Girl. Time to go meet the life changing gurus."

Amber slowly released her grip on the armrests and shakily got to her feet.

When Chet caught sight of her, he bellowed, "See there now, little lady. You did it."

He reached for Amber's hand to help her off the plane. In a comforting, grandfatherly voice, he said to Amber, "Remember what I said to you back there in Cali. You're braver than you know."

And with a quick squeeze to her hand, he guided her onto the dock.

Now that they were all off the plane, Chet turned to Micah and Blair and said, "Okay, Claines, they're all yours. I'll be back in a month with the next food delivery. Good luck, folks."

Those were his departing words to the five guests of Welby Island as he climbed back into Sadie and started the engines.

"Welcome to Welby Island! Micah and I want you to know how thrilled we are that you have chosen the road to enlightenment here at Claine Retreat. However bumpy the road may get in the next three months, you are here to conquer your challenges, and re-enter your God given lives down an astonishingly cleansed path," said the perky red head, Blair.

Because they are such a well-oiled machine, Micah cleared his throat and added, "As Blair, my beautiful, inspirational wife and soul mate has said, you are on a journey now. One that we hope will bring you to terms with your challenges. As your life coaches, we intend to guide you in the right direction. Now with that said, let's begin the journey down the first path. Right this way, please. Grab your things and come along."

Again, Leanne, the Locomotive, was first to move, followed closely by Devon, or rather Devon was closely following Blair, the blazing red head.

Leonard seemed to be keeping a close eye on Amber, so he grabbed her suitcase and said, "Here, let me help you with that."

A still somewhat shell shocked Amber quietly said, "Thank you."

And then there was Rosalie, and she was about to let it be known that she was none too happy about this situation. "Excuse me. Does anyone else notice that I only have on one shoe? Honestly, no parking valet or baggage handlers at that so called airport and now you expect me to schlep down a dock, up a beach, and through a jungle. For the amount of money I paid you, could you not at least offer hotel transportation?" she whined.

Micah and Blair stopped the procession line. Blair turned on her million watt smile and said, "Well, Roseanne, it's like this…"

"It's Rosalie, not Roseanne," Rosalie corrected.

"Yes, I'm sorry. My mistake, Rosalie," said a beaming Blair, "It was very rude of me not to notice that you were hobbling on one four inch heel. Harvey Benton's, right? Please let me offer you some assistance."

Blair walked over to Rosalie, put her hand on Rosalie's arm, bent down, removed the intact Harvey Benton, slipped it off Rosalie's foot, and proceeded to throw it like a boomerang deep into the jungle.

Blair turned to Rosalie with nothing but sugar in her voice and said, "All better, Rachael? Now, let's get a move on. You have a long day ahead of you."

A stunned Rosalie started to say something, but Leanne, the Locomotive, piped in, "Give it up, Drama Queen. Those shoes wouldn't have done you any good in this place. Just watch out for the snakes, spiders, and quick sand."

Feeling pleased, Leanne marched on.

Rosalie grabbed her bags and started forward, but not before she put in the last word, "Bite me, Clothes Hamper." *Hmm…that told her,* thought Rosalie.

Chapter 9

"Seriously, how much farther is this place? I am barefoot, dragging a suitcase, which now has a broken wheel. Honestly, you couldn't have arranged for transportation? I'm pretty sure the thirty thousand dollars I paid *okay Harold paid* for this trip to enlightenment and soul cleansing would have covered a taxi," bitched Rosalie.

She had been complaining non-stop for the entire 15 minute walk. But who could blame her, she was exhausted and her leg was throbbing. Trudging along, she fantasized about who she would kill for just one oxycodone, well, not literally, but like the phrase said, "I would kill for just one more..."

She was snapped out of her fantasy when the blazing redheaded bitch cheerily clapped her hands and announced with dramatic flair, "And here we are! Welcome to Claine Cabin."

Leanne, the Locomotive, stared straight ahead. She blinked frantically, not believing what she saw in front of her.

Leonard and Amber both said, "Huh?" at the same time.

Devon, who has been Blair's biggest fan since they arrived, dropped his bag and said, "What the bloody hell is that?"

Rosalie pulled up the rear, stopped dead in her tracks. Not being one to hold back her thoughts, she blurted out, "No fucking way! Not going to happen! I am a top selling, five tier, gold star, real estate agent, and there is no way I am staying in that, that shack!"

All five of the Welby Island guests concurred.

Leanne, the Locomotive, started up her engine, "This does not look anything like the pictures in the brochure or online. What happened to the two stories, six thousand square foot house, and the wrap around porch with the Adirondack chairs and the built in fire pit?"

Leonard quizzically asked, "I believe I saw in the brochure that there was a therapy pool and a massage gazebo. Would they be, possibly, on the other side of …that?"

Blair and Micah had been prepared for this reaction, but this group was rather feisty, so they needed to take control. "Calm down, everyone. Breathe in, breathe out," Blair said soothingly.

As on cue, Micah piped in and said, "You all know the reason you are here. If we actually had the beautiful house you saw in the brochure, it would only serve as a glorious, relaxing three month vacation, and that my friends, is not why you are here. We have just taken you out of your destructive, lavish lives to submerge you into reality, and the reality is; your lives sucked and you were spiraling down the toilet hole. So, here you are. You will have three months to reflect on exactly what brought you here, and then you can go back to your previous lives, fulfilled and enlightened. All clear now? Great, okay, so I will ask each of you to come forward and hand me your cell phone."

Well, if looks could kill, Micah and Blair would be six feet under right now.

Rosalie, the bull, had her sights set on the red headed matador. She stomped her, scratched and bloody foot twice and took off out of the gate. When she reached Blair, she tackled her, cursing up a sailors streak, "Are you fucking kidding me, you piece of shit? You have thirty thousand of my dollars and I want it back right this minute, do you hear me?"

As Blair was kicking and screaming to Micah to get her off of her, Micah reached for Rosalie and lifted her off Blair, as Devon quickly stepped forward to assist Blair off the ground. Rosalie was still flailing her arms and legs as Micah restrained her.

Blair, having composed herself, marched right up to Rosalie and smacked her clear across the face, and said, "Rebecca, you need to calm down. You are here because you have an addiction to pain pills. Don't make me hurt you because there won't be any Oxycodone in the medicine cabinet."

Rosalie growled and kicked until she could growl and kick no more.

Blair took a deep cleansing breath and continued, "Okay, now that we have all of the histrionics out of the way, why don't we go take a look inside the cabin. You know what they say; don't judge a book by its cover. We'll show you around and then you can take a siesta. Oh, and as for the cell phones, you can keep them. We don't get reception out here on the island, anyway,"

And with a smug smile, she turned toward the cabin with Micah and Devon following closely in her wake.

Rosalie was attempting to reign in her anger when Leanne looked at her and said, "Come on, Pill Popper. Let's go check out our zero star accommodations."

* * *

"Okay. This is not quite as wretched as I thought," said Devon. "How many bedrooms does it have? Do they have their own loo?"

"Well," said Micah, "There are six bedrooms, three downstairs and three upstairs and there is only one bathroom."

He barely got the words out of his mouth before the room erupted.

This time, to the amazement of the other four guests, it was Amber who spoke up and all traces of the warm and fuzzy country bumpkin were gone.

"Oh no, unt uh, that is not going to work. There are five of us, and two of which are not girls. You seriously can't expect the five of us to share one bathroom. Back in Oklahoma, there were seven of us and we only had one bathroom and let me tell you, it was no fun," Amber was starting to hyperventilate, so Leonard reached over and rubbed her back, which led her to dissolve into tears.

"Well," said Micah, they were learning quickly that any sentence starting with 'well' exiting Micah's mouth was not going to be good. "I didn't say we only had one bathroom, I said we only had one bathroom in the house. Actually, there is another bathroom…outside."

All heads shot right following his long bronzed arm as he pointed to the backyard.

"There is an outhouse 50 feet from the back door," he said with such enthusiasm he could have been selling snow to Eskimos.

Blair chirped in, "All right now, why don't you choose your rooms, freshen up, and let's say we all meet back here at six o'clock."

The group of five grumbled something and started off in different directions. Locomotive Leanne made a bee line for the stairs. She had already scoped out the first floor and clearly saw no bathroom. The only other place it could be was up, and that is precisely where she was heading. Once upstairs, she ran for the biggest bedroom, closed the door, and dropped her bag on the bed. As she was surveying her surroundings, she heard voices in the hallway. Grateful she had closed her door, she was tempted to crawl under the covers, and hibernate for three months. That was, until two really hard knocks startled her out of her fantasy. She really, really didn't want to open the door, but she knew she had to if she wanted to get any peace and quiet. Reluctantly, she got off the bed and wrenched open the door. With the Leanne stink eye on high, "What?" she growled.

Rosalie was shouting at Devon, and Devon was shouting at Leanne, "Who says that room is yours!"

Leanne was in no mood for his British bullshit, so she replied with force, "I did. I got here first and in my rule book, that means..."

"What do you mean your rule book? Who died and crowned you Queen?" Devon snarled.

"Well, if you need me to explain it to you in your language, here it is: I, Queen Leanne, have seized this here bedroom, in eminent domain," Leanne said proudly with her chin in the air.

Devon looked at her like she had just downed a bottle of vino and said, "Well, that's just bullocks."

"No, actually, it's not," said a soft voice from behind him. All three of them turned to look at Leonard, with Amber close by his side.

"Ha!" said Leanne, "Now, if you would all just shut the hell up and go find your own rooms that would suit the Queen quite nicely."

And on that note, she turned and went back into her room, and gracefully shut the door.

As on cue, Rosalie grabbed her suitcase and ran straight for the bedroom closest to the bathroom, and, not so gracefully, tripped over her suitcase and slammed her door.

Leonard, Amber, and Devon stared after her.

"Well, this is just bullocks," said Devon.

Leonard cleared his throat and said, "Devon, why don't you and I take the downstairs bedrooms and let the women have the upstairs?"

As on cue, Amber grabbed her bag and dashed into the last bedroom, and politely closed the door.

Devon glared at Boy Wonder and said, "Bloody bullocks is what this is."

He stomped down the stairs like a spoiled three-year-old.

Chapter 10

Blair and Micah arrived back at the cabin around six p.m. Blair was ready to get this show on the road.

"Now that you have had a chance to settle in, it's time for our first meeting," beamed a radiant Blair. "I have drawn up this week's itinerary," she said as Micah passed a copy to each of the guests. "You may divvy up the chores however you like. We will come to the island every Sunday for dinner, here, at the cabin and we'll assess how the week went. At that time…"

"Um, excuse me," Rosalie interrupted, "But I didn't pay you thirty thousand dollars to play house with four whack jobs, and why are you not staying here on the island guiding us down the path of enlightenment?"

"I was just going to ask the same thing," added Leanne, the Locomotive. "Where exactly have you been all day, if you don't stay on the island? And what kind of life coaching, very expensive life coaching, for that matter, is it when you only meet with us once a week?"

Micah and Blair glanced at each other. Micah cleared his throat and said, "Well, first and foremost, we are renowned life coaches and our techniques vary from client to client. In the case of you five, our goal is to have you overcome your challenges in life by reflecting on how you became challenged in the first place. We have grouped you together because we feel, in our professional opinion, that you may be able to help each other. So, with that said, let's go over the weekly chore list, shall we?"

This time it was Devon who spoke up. "You still haven't answered the question of where you spent the last three hours," he said with suspicion.

Exasperated, Blair responded, "If you must know, Micah and I are not only life coaches, we are also trained Naturalists, we…"

Devon sat straight up and gasped, "You're nudists! You've been running around this island naked!"

"Down, boy," said Rosalie, "They said naturalists, not nudists. I believe it has something to do with Mother Nature."

"Well, you're close, Rosie," replied Blair, "But, actually, we incorporate our knowledge of fauna and flora…"

"Whoa, what?" said Devon, "There are other naked people on this island?"

"No," said an annoyed Blair, "They are the trees and flowers, among other things, that surround you in your natural environment that help to renew your energy, but enough of this already…"

Leanne, the Locomotive, started her engine and headed down the track, "Well, don't you think that might be something you should be doing with us? I, for one, know I'd like to renew my energy."

Blair, taking a deep breath to control her annoyance, said, "Absolutely, but in due time. First, we need you to cleanse your mind and soul of your demons. I mean, your challenges, and that happens in steps. So, step one is to embrace your environment and by doing so, you will open your mind to other passages to relieve the stress that caused you to implode, shall we say," said Blair with a million watt, teeth clenching smile.

Oh boy, the steam was coming out of the Locomotive now. "Really?" said Leanne, "That's the first step? Hmm, this list here, looks a lot like a 'honey do' list. Do you know what that is, Blair? Well, let me enlighten you. A 'honey do' list is chores you put upon someone else to complete. And from the looks of this dump, you seem to be asking us to clean it up. Am I close, Red?"

Blair was losing patience with this group. She knew she had to wrap this up quickly so she said sweet as sugar, "Leila dear, this is not a honey do list, as you refer to it. This, here, is the beginning of your journey down the path of enlightenment. We consider it work therapy. If you are busy washing down the decks or hanging laundry out to dry or planting a vegetable

41

garden, you are not thinking of all those reasons that got you to where you are today, so be a dear and go with the flow."

Locomotive Leanne stood, took a few steps closer to Blair, and said, "Okay, Bambi, I'll play your game, but don't think for one minute that I buy your bullshit."

And with that, Leanne, the Locomotive, exited the station.

Chapter 11

Leanne was really, really trying to hold it together, but now sitting on her bed, clutching the picture of the twins, she let the tears flow. Not sure what she was crying about; was it that she was missing her babies, could it be that she actually missed Blake, who gave her the ultimatum of getting help for her issues, or…well, he never actually said 'or', oh, but he implied it. Maybe she was just feeling sorry for herself. Her thoughts were interrupted by a soft knock on the door. Her brain kept saying, 'ignore it, ignore it', but then, the door knob turned.

Amber poked her head through, "Leanne, want to come downstairs? We rustled up some dinner and are about to eat."

"No thanks, I'm not hungry," said Leanne.

Amber moved a little further into the room and said, "Funny, those used to be my favorite words. Every time I had a lunch meeting with my manager or an ad agency, I would order something then push it around on my plate and explain that I'm not all that hungry, which pleased them to punch."

Leanne looked at Amber and said, "So, I guess you're here because you are anorexic or have bulimia."

Amber lowered her head and whispered, "Not exactly."

Leanne, feeling bad for her snide comment, apologized, "I'm sorry, that was really bitchy of me to say."

Amber looked up and said with a shy smile, "Well, you're not that far off. I'm actually here because…"

"You don't have to tell me," Leanne interrupted.

"No, no, it's okay. To be honest with you, I kind of got myself into this pickle. You see, I was trying really hard to fit in with the Hollywood crowd. When my agent suggested that I start being seen out and about with some celebrities, said it would be good for my career, she introduced me to a guy named Joe. He is a model and a client of hers. She thought that it would be a perfect match. However, that is not exactly what happened. Joe ran with a celebrity crowd. Boy was he good looking, but we were just from two different worlds. However, he must have gotten pressure from Ellen, our agent, so he dragged me around to all of these wild parties and night clubs. On our third night out, Joe asked me to come with him to a party, said I would meet some really important people, so I did. Well, that's where I kind of fell off track. I walked into the party and immediately felt out of place. Joe swept into the room like he owned it. About an hour later, he told me to follow him into this room, which I did. There were about 15 people in there, all gathered around a table full of cocaine. They offered me some and I said, "No, thank you," but Joe pulled me aside and said that if I wanted to fit in, I had to play the game. We went back to the table and I did a line, and then proceeded to sneeze all over the table, taking with it all the stuff on the table. Well, that went over like a fox in the hen house. Anyway, I thought that would be the last I would see of Joe and that crowd, but it wasn't. After four months of being out and about, seen on Joe's arm every night of the week and weekends, I just plumb got worn out. I looked like what the cat dragged in and the work stopped coming. That is when Gio called me to his office and suggested me coming here. The worst part is, he believed that I had a cocaine problem. And truth be told, I let him think it. I never told him that I hated all the late nights at the clubs and parties, because I was afraid of missing my 'big break'."

Leanne sat quiet, at a loss for words.

Amber sat on the edge of the bed to compose herself. As she did, she reached out for the frame lying next to her. When she looked at it, she said to Leanne, "My goodness, are these your two babies? They are just the cutest little things I've ever seen."

Leanne took a deep breath and said, "Yes, that's Luke and Lindsey, and I'm afraid they are not so little or babies anymore. They just turned six and started first grade this year."

"Well, I can see with my own eyes how much you are missing them, so here's my two cents. Let's go downstairs and eat, so we can both get on that path of enlightenment and you can get home to your babies."

Amber linked arms with Leanne like Dorothy and the Tin Man skipping down the yellow brick road, and headed for the door.

When Amber and Leanne entered the kitchen, the other three turned, and looked at them. "Okay, ya'll. The gurus want us to find enlightenment, then enlightenment we shall find, and the sooner the better. So we can all get the heck off this island," said Amber with authority.

And with that said, they picked up their forks and dug in.

After five minutes of silence, Rosalie pushed her plate away and said, "I'm not one for nice words unless it involves you buying a ten million dollar house. And since that is not the case here, I am going on record, that meal sucked. I'm not saying that to be mean. I'm saying it because I think we are in real trouble here if that was the effort of four out of five of us. Apparently, none of us can cook."

Devon shot right back at Rosalie, "Hey, Pill Popper. I have been a bachelor all my days and have cooked for myself numerous times, and I survived."

Rosalie volleyed back, "Really, Rock Star? You cook all your own meals? No, I'm thinking you're confusing cooking your own meals with having a cook to make your meals, or maybe one of your pop tarts has some skills outside the bedroom."

Devon pushed his plate back and leaned forward across the table into Rosalie's space and with steely eyes and a clenched jaw, said slowly, "What the bloody hell do you know about me? You are nothing but a sniveling, whining…"

Leanne, having heard enough, said in her best stern mother voice, "Okay! That's enough, you two. If you have nothing nice to say, then say nothing at all. Don't make me have to separate you two."

When she finished, all eyes were on her.

Amber, trying not to laugh, said, "Leanne, I think you just scolded the children." With that, Amber and Leanne broke down in laughter.

Leonard, holding back for as long as he could, joined them. Devon and Rosalie, not finding this amusing, sat back, folded their arms, and watched the other three laugh until tears flowed down their cheeks.

Rosalie, having had enough, said, "Can we please get back to the original point of this conversation, which is obviously none of us can cook. And I, for one, don't care, too."

Leanne, using her napkin to wipe away the tears of laughter, said, "Okay, okay, Rosalie is right, but no worries. I can cook, and I actually enjoy it, so I'll take on cooking the meals from here on, deal?"

All heads nodded in agreement.

Chapter 12

Devon woke to the sound of pots clanking and hens clucking. The hens being the three women: Leanne, Rosalie, and Amber. He tried flipping onto his stomach and putting the pillow over his head; that didn't work. He grabbed the covers and pulled them over his head; that didn't work. Fighting a losing battle, he threw his feet out of bed, grumbled, "Bloody hell."

He pulled on his jeans and headed for the bathroom. Unfortunately, he had to pass through the kitchen to get there. He was about to make his way out back to the so called second bathroom, a.k.a. outhouse, when he stopped dead in his tracks, sniffed the air, and said, ""Do I smell crumpets?"

All three women looked at him.

Amber asked, "What's a crumpet?"

Before Devon could answer, Rosalie piped in and said, "No, that glorious smell is pancakes. Apparently, Locomotive is an amazing cook."

Devon continued sniffing around the kitchen like a hound dog, "Whoa, is that bangers I smell and brewed coffee?"

Again, Amber said, "What's a banger?"

Rosalie clarified, "Well, yes, Horn Dog, that would be sausage. Are you going to continue to sniff out your breakfast or give us a hand setting the table?"

On that note, Devon said, "Yeah, okay, I have to hit the loo. I'll be right back."

He dashed out the back door and across the lawn.

Amber turned to Rosalie and said, "Huh?"

"He had to go to the little boy's room," explained Rosalie.

"Oh, got it," said the Country Bumpkin, and all three women laughed. Just then, Leonard came through back the door with a basket of wild berries.

"What the hell took you so long, Whiz Kid?" said the Locomotive, "I've been waiting 45 minutes for those berries."

Leonard placed the berries on the counter and said, "Those berries are not easy to pick. Look at my hands. I look like I lost a fight with a bag of cats."

Amber instinctively ran over to Leonard and led him to the sink to clean up the scratches. Rosalie and Leanne glanced at each other and smiled.

The back door slammed and Devon raced in, "You didn't start eating yet, did you?"

Leanne shook her head and said, "No, Romeo. Wash your hands and set the table."

As Devon, Leonard, and Amber got the plates and utensils, Rosalie washed the berries. Leanne whipped the cream by hand, grumbling, "God forbid there be a mixer in this dump."

She and Rosalie brought the platters of pancakes, sausage, and berries to the table. Amber followed with a carafe of coffee, or more accurate, a thermos found in the cabinet, and a jug of orange juice.

After 15 minutes of complete silence, Amber pushed her plate away, and declared, "Yum, yum, yummy. Even though my momma is the best baker this side of the Mississippi, she would be dang proud of you, Leanne."

As always, the polite boy, Leonard, concurred.

Devon belched loudly and said, "Not bad, Queenie."

Rosalie could barely move; she was so full. She turned to the men and said, "We women, cooked. You men, clean."

Devon raised an eyebrow and said, "Is that stated on the weekly chore chart?"

Locomotive Leanne casually replied, "Well, if you ever want to eat again, I suggest you don't argue. Speaking of that asinine chore chart, maybe we should take a look at it and see what the insightful life coaches have in mind."

After the table was cleared and the dishes washed, and dried, the five grabbed their coffee and headed out back to sit in the rare Washington spring sunshine.

"Okay," Leonard adjusted his glasses, and began, "I have analyzed this chore chart and my perception is; if we all pool together our abilities, we can make this happen. There are ten weekly chores, if we each take two; we can manage."

Everyone nodded in agreement.

Leanne spoke first, "Okay, these are the ten chores: Laundry, cooking, dish duty, cleaning, gardening, mowing, hosing down the decks, painting the house; what the fuck, are they delusional; window washing, and pest control. What the fuck does that mean? Okay, so we all know I am on cooking duty, who wants laundry?"

Dead silence.

"Okay," Leanne said, "We can do this the easy way, or the hard way."

Amber stepped up and said, "I guess I can do the gardening, seeing as I grew up on a farm."

"Good, that's good," said Leanne, "Okay, anyone else?"

"Oh hells bells! How hard can it be to wash sheets and towels? I'll take laundry," said Rosalie, but quickly added, "We all do our own personal items. I'm not laying my hands on anyone else's skivvies."

"Okay, agreed," Leanne concurred and everyone nodded. "Since I'm cooking, I would like someone else to do the dishes, any volunteers?"

Dead silence.

"Really, people? I am two seconds away from putting this list in a bowl and whatever you pick, is what you get, and no do overs allowed. So, decide now; would you rather choose or be chosen?"

Devon sighed and said, "I'll take dishes."

All four heads turned and said, "Really?" at the same time.

"What?" said an irked Devon, "I've been a bachelor all my life. I know how to rinse a pot and soak a dish."

"Well, actually, it's more like, soak a pot and rinse a dish, but who's splitting hairs. You're up, Rock Star. No pun intended," said an amused Leanne.

"Oh, you're a funny one, Queen Bee. Let's see how much laughing you'll be doing without your liter of wine."

Ut oh, the Locomotive was back on the tracks. The death glare would have brought the bravest of men to their knees, but Devon held her eyes.

"Okay, you two, as much as I would like to buy tickets to this show, this isn't the time for a Wild West showdown. Bottle it up and save it for a rainy day," said an amused Rosalie and then added, "No pun intended, Leanne."

That brought Rosalie into a fit of laughter, which in turn got Amber going. Leonard held back for as long as he could until the dam burst. The three of them were laughing so hard that Rosalie had to make a run for the outhouse before she wet her pants.

When Rosalie returned, a defeated Leanne said, "Well, I'm glad you all got a good laugh at our expense. Devon, would you like to take a bow?"

She grabbed his hand, stood him up, and curtsied. Catching on, he turned to the audience and bowed. Upon completion, they both flipped the amused roomies, the bird.

"Okay. Let's get this done," said Leanne, "Who wants mowing?"

Dead silence.

"Oh for Christ sake! I'll take mowing since I'll need to get out of the kitchen, once in a while. Plus, I could use the exercise."

"Um, please don't take this the wrong way, Leanne," said a shy Leonard, "But have you ever mowed grass before?"

"Yup, I'm the jack of all trades, just ask my A-hole husband. Okay, so we have cooking, laundry, gardening, and mowing covered. What's left is cleaning, and that doesn't mean picking up other people's shit. It's keeping the floors, bathroom, kitchen, and whatever you call that other room clean."

"I'll take it," said Leonard. "I'm kind of a neat freak so it's a win-win for me."

"You know, Leonard, I just realized we don't know why you're here, and honestly, I have been trying to figure it out, but I'm stumped," said Rosalie.

Looking nervous, Leonard replied, "Aren't we suppose to reveal that in group with Blair and Micah?"

"Ha!" snorted Rosalie, "We are the group, Einstein. As smart as you are, you're not seeing the writing on the wall. Those two sociopaths aren't going to do diddly shit for us. Their banking our money and were banking on our odds that A: We'll survive the three months, and B: Not end up worse than when we landed on this God forsaken island."

Leonard knew she was right, but he really didn't want them to know what a mess he had made of his life. But it was inevitable, because here he was on Welby Island.

"Leonard," Amber said softly, "I don't think any of us are proud to be here, but we are for one reason or another. Once I told Leanne how I ended up here, being something to do with cocaine, I felt so much better. I know it may be hard to believe, but Leanne is really nice when she wants to be. Sorry, Leanne."

"No worries, Country Bumpkin. I know I'm a bitch. That's one of the things I am going to try and work on," said Leanne, sincerely.

Devon and Rosalie's jaws hit the ground. "You Barbie, as innocent as a babe in a pram, are here because you have a cocaine addiction. Oh that's priceless," laughed Devon.

Rosalie recovered herself and smacked Devon on the head and said, "Zip it, perv."

She turned to Amber and said in an alien voice, "Sweetie, how old are you?"

Amber looked at Leonard, then at Leanne, and said with her head held high, "Twenty one."

"Oh sweet, baby Jesus," said a stunned Rosalie. Then she turned to Leonard and said, "Spill it."

Leonard looked around nervously, but when he landed on Amber's cornflower blue eyes, he blurted out, "Gambling!"

"I knew it!" shouted Devon, "I have been picking up the betting innuendos. I said to myself if I was a betting bloke, I would have to say, Boy Wonder, here, is a betting bloke himself. So let me ask you, Boy Genius, how did you lose all of your mum and dad's money? Horses, Football, Poker?"

"Well, that may not have been the problem," said a coy Leonard, "You see I didn't lose anything, I kept winning in Vegas. They thought I was fixing the tables somehow, but couldn't prove it. So, they banned me."

"Huh?" said the quartet.

"Listen, can we save this for another session and get back on track with the chores list?" said a determined Leanne.

And so they did. Cleaning and deck washing went to Leonard, house painting and dish washing went to Devon, gardening and pest control, whatever that entails, went to

Amber, laundry and window washing to Rosalie, and cooking and mowing to the Locomotive.

Chapter 13

Amber pushed through the back door of the house covered in mud and carrying two sacks of vegetables. "I swear, I think someone just threw seeds into the dirt and hoped something would grow. That garden is a mess! I've spent this entire week pulling weeds and cutting back plants," said Amber exasperatedly.

Leanne, standing at the stove stirring something that smelled fabulous, turned to get a good look at Amber, and said, "Country Bumpkin, you look like you've been playing in a mud puddle."

"I have!" squealed Amber, "Honestly, Leanne, I don't know who planted that garden, but they sure didn't know what they were doing."

Amused, Leanne said, "Let's see what you have in the sacks."

Amber went over to the sink and dumped both sacks, and began washing the vegetables. Frustrated, she said to Leanne, "I'm not sure what all this is, but I just kept picking stuff that looked edible. If my daddy saw that mess of a garden, he'd have a cow."

Leanne picked up the rinsed vegetables and said, "Okay, let's see what we have here; these are beets, and these are scallions, these over here are supposed to be peas, but not quite mature enough yet. Oh my God, Amber, you did great."

Leanne picked up a green with a long white root, smelled it, and said, "This is wild garlic, and the long stringy things are pole beans, and I believe you hit the jackpot with these," Leanne held up some green leafy things, "This is spinach, this is red leaf lettuce, and this is basil."

Amber wasn't quite sure why Leanne was so happy, but beamed at her and said, "Thanks, Leanne. I didn't have a clue of what I was picking, but now I'll know what to look for next time."

Leanne gently laid the vegetables on four dish towels to dry. She went back to the stove and stirred the pot.

Amber stepped up beside her and said, "Yum, that smells great, what are you making?"

Leanne smiled and said, "I'm calling it, everything but the kitchen sink soup. I usually like to cook from scratch; make my own broth from roasted chickens, but I found canned broth in the pantry and today, Devon found a box freezer in the garage full of frozen food, so I am just winging it. However, now that you have brought me this garden booty, I can add some fresh herbs."

Feeling pleased, Amber declared, "Well, let me tell you, those gurus don't deserve all of your effort here, but I for one, am truly grateful."

"Oh, trust me, I'm not doing this for fric and frac. If I had it my way, they wouldn't be coming for dinner," said the Locomotive.

"I know. This should be real interesting tonight. I mean, we haven't seen or heard from them this whole week and then they just show up on Sunday night like they have a reservation at a fancy restaurant," Amber said, as she poured herself a glass of ice tea, and then after taking a long thirsty gulp, she screamed, "Leanne! Is there mint in this tea?"

A startled Leanne responded cautiously, "Yes, I found some growing along the side of the house when I was mowing. Why, are you allergic to mint?"

"No, no, nothing like that," said Amber after she gulped down the rest, "It's just that, when I was a little girl and feeling blue, my momma would make me a cup of hot tea and add mint in it to soothe me," explained Amber with tears in her eyes.

Leanne walked over to Amber and wrapped her arms around her and said in a thick voice, "I know, sweetie. I do that for my babies, when they have upset tummies."

Just then, Rosalie rushed into the kitchen and said, "What the devil is going on in here? It sounded like a cat got its tail caught in the door."

She stopped dead in her tracks and said, "Is someone hurt? Why are you two crying?"

Leanne and Amber swiped at their tears, and Leanne said, "No, no one is hurt. We were just having a bout of nostalgia."

Leanne turned back to the stove and stirred the pot.

Rosalie looked at them skeptically and said, "Wow, it smells fantastic in here."

Devon and Leonard walked in.

Well, the gang's all here, thought Leanne.

Horn Dog's nose was on high alert, and he said, "What is that amazing aroma?"

Then Leonard said, "Is that homemade soup? I've never had homemade soup, as in made in our house. My mother was not one for culinary accomplishments, so that meant a lot of eating out or the occasional take in."

Stunned, Leanne and Amber said at the same time, "Really?"

Rosalie piped in, "Me too, Boy Wonder."

Leanne and Amber both said, "What?"

"Nope. When I was young, it came from a can, if we were lucky. My father was a deadbeat and left when I was four. My mother worked three jobs, so no home cooking nostalgia for me," said a somber Rosalie.

Leanne, treading lightly asked, "You said 'we'. Do you have siblings?"

Rosalie bent down and rubbed her leg, not looking at Leanne replied, "A brother, but he died."

Amber and Leanne looked at each other and then Leanne, not wanting to dig any deeper, said, "I guess we'll leave that one on the table for the renowned life coaches, which speaking of, will be here in two hours. I need to get this bread baked and grab a quick shower, so everyone out of the kitchen."

Amber, feeling more composed, said, "Well, I definitely need a shower. I look like I've been wrestling swine in the pen. I'll go first and make it a quickie, as to save you some hot water."

As Amber exited the room, Rosalie turned to Devon, and said, "Down, boy. She didn't mean that kind of quickie."

Rosalie left the kitchen.

Devon was really starting to get annoyed with these females and said to the two remaining people in the room,

Leonard and Leanne, "Why does my willy have to be the butt of all jokes to you hens?"

And with that, Leanne and Leonard lost it.

"Oh bloody hell," said a pissed off Devon as he slammed out the back door.

Leonard composed himself and turned to Leanne, "Do you need any help in the kitchen?"

"No, I'm good, thanks," said Leanne.

Leonard headed out back to apologize to Devon.

Chapter 14

The table was set. Leanne was fussing nervously around the kitchen when Devon walked in, and helped himself to a piece of bread. Leanne glared at him and said, "That was rude."

Devon ignored her and helped himself to another piece of bread. Leanne, the Locomotive, snatched it out of his hand, and said snidely, "What part of rude don't you understand?"

Devon returned her glare and said smugly, "Someone's jonesing for a glass of wine. What was your go to? Wait! Let me guess; Chardonnay, that always seems to be the choice for all the high society, stick up their ass, women I've ever known."

Leanne counted to ten, like she did with the twins when they are pushing her buttons, and calmly said, "And how many high society women did you fuck? Oh, wait. Let me guess; two. The other nine-hundred were 18-year-old, raging hormone groupies."

As the two of them continued to glare at one another, the back door swung open, and in walked Micah and Blair. Leanne turned her back on them and Devon greeted them with a grunt.

"Good evening, Evan and Lena," said Blair cheerfully.

Then Micah said brightly, "Wow, something smells incredible."

Just then, they were joined by Leonard, Amber, and Rosalie.

"Wonderful, you're all here," said Blair.

Rosalie, not missing a beat, replied, "And where did you think we would actually be, Red, swimming to the mainland?"

Blair considered that for a moment and said, "Well, Rhonda, I wouldn't be surprised if you attempted it. But with that banged up leg of yours, you wouldn't get far. But enough of this, we are here, and eager to discuss how your first week went."

With that said, Blair plopped down into the closest chair.

Leanne turned to the group and said, "Everyone sit. The sooner we get this enlightenment soiree over with, the sooner these two can skedaddle back to the hole they crawled out of."

The silence in the room was eventually broken when Leonard said, "Hi, Blair. Hi, Micah."

Amber followed suit with a good ole country, "Hi, ya'll."

She went to the fridge to retrieve the pitcher of tea.

Once everyone was seated, Leanne brought over the pot of soup and placed it in the middle of the table, turned back to retrieve a piping hot loaf of herb focaccia bread, then grabbed a seat next to Amber. She looked around the table and said in astonishment, "Don't look at me like that. No way am I ladling soup into your bowls, it's a DIY dinner."

With that said, she proceeded to help herself.

The others followed and everyone ate in silence. Blair daintily wiped her mouth with her napkin and said, "What an odd choice for an appetizer. But I must say, it was very good. I hope the entrée is just as good, and vegan."

Oh shit, Locomotive Leanne was revving her engine and aiming straight for the red head.

Amber quickly spoke up, "Blair, Leanne is an amazing cook, and we are always happy with what she makes. We aren't a fancy schmancy L.A. restaurant, so we don't eat courses. We are more of a pot luck kind of crowd, so consider yourself lucky to have been served a pot of homemade soup."

Holy crap, Leanne shut down her engines and said, "Thank you, Amber. Now let's all hope we don't lose our appetite for dessert after the gurus here enlighten us. So, Blair, why don't you guys say your spiel and then you can be on your merry way back to the mainland."

Micah was on bowl number two of the delicious soup when Blair kicked him under the table. He let out a little yelp of 'ow' and then cleared his throat and said, "Well, okay then. We would like to start with the chore chart. How did you all decide who would do what?"

This time it was Leonard who spoke up, "Well, Micah, we as a group, decided that we would each take two chores; being that the list consisted of ten…"

Micah interrupted and said, "Yes, yes, I'm very well aware of how many chores were on the list, but what we are asking you is, how did you decide who took which?"

All eyes were on Leonard. Devon pushed back from the table, leaned back in his chair, crossed his arms, and began to smile slowly. He was watching Leonard closely and what he saw was a poker face, so he knew this would be good. Amber stared wide eyed at him, wondering what he was up to. Rosalie and Leanne glanced at each other and held their breath.

Blair, sounding a bit impatient, said, "Yes, please, do tell how you divided the chores."

Leonard stood, went into the living room, and returned with deck of cards. He sat back down, pulled out the deck, shuffled, and began, "Well, as you know, there isn't much night life out here at Claine Cabin, so we have to find ways to entertain ourselves. At first, the discussion of divvying up the chores became heated, so we had to find a way to assign them fair and square. Picking out of a bowl was too boring, so we opted for strip poker," said Leonard with the straightest poker face, and then added, "You see it was a win-win for Devon and I. And these ladies," moving his eyes toward the hens, "Well, they were all for it."

Breathing like the big bad wolf, Blair exploded, "Are you fucking kidding me! You played strip poker to choose your chores!"

Leonard, still in character, said, "Why, yes, Blair. That's what I'm saying, and it worked out very well for me, considering, I'm an ace poker player, and didn't lose so much as a sock."

Blair, rendered speechless, looked around the table, and was greeted with ear to ear smiles from the five guests of Claine Cabin. Amber, having caught on to where this was going, chimed in, "I was so lucky I lost all of my clothes first, because I got to pick gardening, which suits me to a T."

Next, it was Devon who spoke up. "As it did me, Country Girl," he said with a cheeky smile.

Blair had had enough, she stood, glaring down at the five of them, and hissed, "You think this is a game...well, let me tell you, you won't be laughing when you leave here if you keep this up." She turned to a wide eyed Micah and said, "Come."

And out the back door, they stormed.

Leanne was the first to speak, "Holy shit, Brainiac, what came over you?"

Rosalie was next to comment, "Boy Wonder, you amaze me."

Then Devon concluded with, "Well done, mate. The look on Blair's face was priceless."

Amber, at a loss for words, just smiled.

Leonard, not use to 'Atta boy's', blushed like a school boy.

"Okay," said Leanne gleefully, "Who wants some humble pie?"

The room erupted in laughter.

After indulging in the delicious wild berry pie, Amber sat back, and declared, "That was the best pie I have ever had, and that's saying a lot, after growing up on my momma's apple crumble."

Pleased, Leanne said, "Thank you, Country Bumpkin."

Leonard, feeling lucky after his performance, said, "Anyone up for a game of strip poker?"

The room erupted in laughter.

Devon quick on his feet said, "I'm up for it," which sent the hens into a cackling fit of laughter. "Okay, okay," said an amused Devon, "That may have been a bad choice of words, but I think a friendly game of five-card Monte is a grand idea. I'll clean up in here and meet you all in the living room."

As the others filed out, Leanne hung back, packing away the leftovers. She hesitated, but then thought, *oh what the hell,* and said to Devon's back, "Um, listen, Romeo, I want to apologize for snapping at you earlier. I know we all have our issues to deal with, but you seem to be taking the brunt of our frustrations, so, um...well, I'll work on controlling my mouth."

Devon rinsed a plate, grabbed the drying towel, and turned to lean against the sink. He continued drying the plate, looking directly at Leanne, and said, "Um, well, I don't believe I have been very considerate of your feelings either. So what do you say to a truce, Queen Bee?"

Leanne, feeling a little flutter in her belly, said, "I think that's a fine idea, Rock Star. How about I help you finish cleaning and then we go knock the socks off of baby Einstein."

Chapter 15

It was one of those rare blue sky, warm, sunshine days on the island. Even though the nights were still quite chilly, 72 degrees, and sunshine is a gift the three hens truly deserved. It's been three weeks since they landed on Welby Island and the days were dragging by. Rosalie was spread out on a blanket doing yoga and Leanne was in the rickety old hammock that threatened to collapse at any moment, reading the novel she brought.

Amber was up to her elbows weeding the garden, she turned to the hens and said, "Ya'll, do you think Micah and Blair are ever going to come back? It's been two weeks since our last meeting and they left pretty angry."

Rosalie, from her downward dog position, said, "Who cares."

Leanne responded, "Not me, truthfully. I think we are surviving better than if we had them breathing down our necks, preaching enlightenment."

Amber stood up and brushed off her knees, "I agree, Leanne. But honestly, don't you think they should be doing their job; the job we paid a pretty penny for?"

Leanne put her book down, sat up to look at Amber, and said, "Yes, I do, if that was what they were intending. But I've got to tell you, I have a pretty good bullshit radar and it went on high alert the minute I met them. My only concern is we are starting to run low on supplies and Chet won't be here for another seven days."

Rosalie slowly descended from her position, grabbed her water bottle, took a large gulp, and said, "What kind of supplies are we low on, and please don't say toilet paper?"

At that moment, Leonard and Devon emerged from the woods and on cue, Rosalie said, "Speaking of," and all three hens cackled.

When Devon and Leonard reached them, their arms loaded with firewood, Leonard said, "Hello, ladies."

Devon inquired, "What's so funny? And, please, for the love of the Queen, do not say it was about me. I have had enough hen-pecking to last me a lifetime."

Leanne looked over at him and said, "You and I have a truce, but I have no control over the other hens."

Amber had just finished loading the vegetables into a sack, walked over to the others, and said, "Why don't you guys go unload the firewood. I'll bring these inside, wash them, and then, I'll bring out a pitcher of cold tea."

Feeling confident she added, "I'd like to call a meeting, if ya'll are okay with that."

Rosalie and Leanne glanced at each other.

Leonard said, "Sure, that sounds great," and headed inside.

Devon shrugged and said, "I could use a cold tea after lugging this firewood. Be back in a minute."

Amber followed them both into the house. Rosalie wiped her sweaty forehead and said to Leanne, "What do you think that's about?"

"I'm not sure," responded Leanne, as she got off the hammock. "I've been noticing this past week that she's not as perky as she has been. I think sometimes we overlook the fact that she's a 21-year-old country girl, who has been living in the Hollywood scene; trying to fit in. Let's wait and hear what she has on her mind," said a concerned Leanne.

Ten minutes later, all five were gathered around the worn out picnic table, drinking cold tea, and munching on leftover cookies from the night before.

Amber was twisting the life out of her napkin, so Leanne spoke up, "Amber, do have something on your mind that you would like to talk about?"

Amber was feeling vulnerable. The same feeling she would get when she walked into an audition, but she kept repeating Mr. Chet's words in her head, "You're braver than you know, you're braver than you know."

She straightened her back, dropped her napkin, and said, "Yes, yes I do. I know we all came here to this island for a reason, but we've been here for three weeks and not one of us has said boo about them. So, I was wondering, since the gurus seemed to have washed their hands of us, if maybe, we could all have our own meeting and talk about why we are here?"

The other four looked at each other, then at Amber, but nobody said a word. Seeing that maybe this was a bad idea, Amber quickly back pedaled and said, "I'm sorry, I didn't mean to make ya'll uncomfortable. Just forget I said a thing."

Rosalie took a sip of her tea and said, "No, you're right, Amber. I, for one, would like to stop fighting this by myself. So, here it is, this is my story."

Rosalie talked non-stop for a half an hour, explaining, how after tripping over the Virgin Mary and breaking her leg, she got hooked on pain pills. When she was finished, she took a deep breath and said, "Shit, that felt good," and wiped away the few tears that escaped.

Devon, not very well equipped to deal with female emotions, decided to lighten the moment and announced to Rosalie, "Maybe I can help you with your ache. I've been told by more than a few lassies that I am pretty good with my hands."

Rosalie looked at him, then at his hands, and replied, "That's not where my ache is, Horn Dog."

Devon looking a little flustered said, "Well, I know that...I was talking about massaging your bloody leg."

That sent the table into a fit of laughter.

Feeling slightly more confident Amber said, "So, anyone else?"

Dead silence.

Everyone seemed to be looking for something at the bottom of their glass. Not letting them defeat her she said, "Fine, I'll go. Rosalie, thank you, I know firsthand how hard that was for you. I truly appreciate you sharing your story."

Amber took a deep breath and began, "Okay, I'm not going to sugar coat this. I was struggling to land modeling and acting jobs, even though my agent was constantly telling me that the next gig was a sure thing. Well, over and over again, it certainly was not a sure thing. So, she thought maybe it would be good for my career if I was seen out and about on the town with some, as she called them, Hollywood bad boys. She set me up with another of her clients, Joe, who was a model. We went out and about to clubs and parties every night of the week and every weekend. Being a girl from a small town, I, for the life of me, cannot understand why people need to go out every single night of the week. Anyway…"

Amber went on for another 20 minutes, with all eyes riveted on her. By the time she was done, she blew out a breath, and with tears streaking down her cheeks, she said, "When I saw those pictures and asked Gio who she was, I truthfully did not recognize that it was me."

Leonard, not wanting to see Amber hurt, blurted out, "To hell with them! I think you are beautiful."

Stunned at his own words, he looked away in shyness.

Amber composed herself. Looked right into Leonard's thick, black, bottle lens, glass covered eyes and said sweetly, "Thank you."

Leanne snuck a peek at Devon and quickly looked away, but apparently, not quite quick enough. He turned to her and said with some compassion, "How about you, Queen Bee? You have the most to lose when we get off this bleeping island. Maybe it's time you lowered your armor and tell us all how an amazing cook like you ended drowning in a vat of vino?"

Leanne looked at him, and then at the others. Realizing that she actually did have a lot to lose if she didn't come to grips with why she was on this island. So she took a deep breath and began, "To be truthful with you all, I don't know where to begin. But I have had some time to think about it and I guess it began when my husband, Blake, became a partner in his firm three years ago."

And from there the Locomotive traveled down the tracks telling her story of her feelings of being lost and alone, sad and unhappy, the stress of practically being a single parent to twins. When Leanne finished, she blew out a breath and reached for her napkin to wipe away her tears, which now flowed unstoppable.

Leonard quietly asked, "Leanne, why didn't you tell Blake that you only had two glasses of wine when he accused you of drinking the bottle and passing out?

Leanne looked at Leonard, shook her head, and replied, "I don't know. I guess I didn't have it in me to defend myself. Blake is an attorney and he never loses, or at least, when we fought. I was lying out there under the stars the night before, searching for the answer as to why I was so unhappy. And when he confronted me the next morning and accused me of being drunk, I just let him believe it. He knows I am not a big drinker, but I thought maybe he might be concerned and would want to hear why I was so miserably exhausted and unhappy. However, that was not the case. His solution was to hire a nanny to take care of the kids if I couldn't..." Tears welling up in her eyes, Leanne stopped talking.

Amber quickly got up from her seat, ran around the table, and hugged Leanne from behind, her own tears soaking Leanne's hair. Rosalie, sitting next to Leanne, leaned in and grabbed her hand. Devon and Leonard looked away in silence.

After a few minutes, giving them time to compose themselves, Devon cleared his throat and said, "Leanne, maybe if I was lucky enough to find someone as lovely as you, I would stop waving my willy at every skirt that crossed my path." With that said, the trio of hens turned into a huddle of giggles.

Leanne smiled at Devon and said softly, "Thank you."

Devon clapped his hands together and stood up, "All righty then. I think we have made huge strides today. Why don't we call it a day, and move along."

In unison, the hens clucked, "Oh no. Not so fast, Romeo."

Rosalie said to Devon, "Having to come to this island was one of the worst things I thought could happen to me, but hearing your story will make it all worthwhile. So, spill it, Horn Dog."

Even though Devon was a famous Rock Star, ironically, he has never been comfortable in the spot light. So, with four pairs of eyes staring at him, he began to squirm. Seeing no way around it, he began, "Um, well, okay. You see, I just happen to fancy women. However, I ended up in this quandary, because I came very close to playing romper room with the L.A. Chief of Police's 16-year-old daughter; so, in return for not sending me to jail, my manager offered up a stint here at the Claine Enlightenment Retreat. So here I am, end of story."

The hens were quiet, not a cluck to be heard, even though their mouths were wide open. Rosalie, unlatched her hand from Leanne's and said, "You mean to tell us that you were almost about to have sex with Chief O'Rourke's 16-year-old daughter, Kelsey? Oh my God! That is priceless. I have known Tommy O'Rourke for 15 years. Little Kelsey was only a year-old. All I can say, Romeo is, that you got off easy. Kelsey is the apple of her daddy's eye. I am truly surprised you do not have bullet holes in you. Sweet baby Jesus, that is classic."

Devon, seeing an out from telling his whole story, decided to play along with Rosalie's amusement, "Yes, very well, now. I am so glad I could entertain you. But now, I think it's time we move on to Boy Wonder over here. As like you Rosalie, Leonard here's story, I'm sure, will make it worth it for me. So, let's hear it, Boy Genius."

Leonard looked like he was going to puke or pass out. Not knowing how to get out of telling his embarrassing story, especially in front of Amber, he said quietly, "Could I have a pass? I'm really not feeling so well."

Amber, seeing the fear in his eyes, walked back around the table, and sat down next to him, and took his clammy hand in hers, and said, "Leonard, the way you put those gurus in their place that night, showed all of us what a good person you are. Whatever you did to end up here can be nothing short of brilliant, so for me, won't you share a part of yourself with us?"

Okay, he thought, *here is the biggest gamble of your life, Leonard.*

He took a deep breath and began. Thirty minutes later, after telling about how he got banned from Vegas, then creating his own casino in the basement of his parent's multi-million dollar company, about Frankie Baby, and the grannies, he held his breath and waited for the others reactions. Most importantly, Ambers.

Devon, who could no longer contain himself, burst out laughing. He turned to Leonard and said, "Leonard, my man, you are brilliant. I, for one, can honestly say I am proud to have met you. And if it hadn't been for the grannies, you would have been on your way to making a killing. You and I are going to talk, my friend. I seriously have some terrific ideas for video games."

"Ha! I bet you do," said Leanne and Rosalie at the same time and that brought the table to a roar of laughter.

Leanne, feeling lighter then she had in a long time, stood to stretch, and said, "There is one more thing we need to discuss. It's been two weeks since the life coaches have graced us with their presence. Chet and Sadie won't be here with the food delivery for another seven days. The garden is flourishing, thanks to Amber, but we need to find another food source. Any ideas?"

Devon got up and stretched, then said, with a cheeky smile, "As a matter of fact, I think I do."

Chapter 16

Leanne woke the following morning feeling refreshed. She looked at her watch and shot straight up. "What the hell," she said as she scrambled out of bed. She couldn't remember the last time she had slept in until nine a.m. She hurried into the bathroom to brush her teeth and then hastily dressed, hoping along the way that the others were still asleep. Pulling her hair back into a pony tail, she scurried into the kitchen and stopped dead in her tracks. She could not believe her eyes. Devon was at the stove with an apron on, Rosalie was at the sink washing something, and Amber and Leonard were sitting at the perfectly set table with their heads close together. When she finally found her voice, Leanne said, "What in the world! I can't remember the last time I slept until nine a.m."

"Amen to that," said a chirpy Rosalie.

Leanne stepped further into the kitchen and said, "I'm sorry, what can I do to help?"

Devon wiped his hands on his apron and smiled at her, "Don't fret, Queen Bee. We thought we would give you the morning off. Sit."

With that said, he handed her a steaming mug of coffee. She did as she was told, however, feeling guilty.

"Okay, everyone. Let's eat," said a jubilant Devon and on that note, he set down a platter of eggs, bangers, and potatoes. Rosalie followed close behind with a bowl of fresh berries.

Leanne ate another fork full of eggs and then said to Devon, "So, Romeo, where did you learn to cook? These eggs and potatoes are really good."

Devon took the last bite, wiped his mouth, pushed his plate away, and replied, "Well, as you all know, I'm a musician. However, in my humbling beginnings, I had to work odd jobs to support myself. When I was 17, I worked as a short order cook at a local pub in Mousehole…"

Amber put down her fork and said, "You lived in a town called Mousehole?"

Amused, Devon replied, "That's right, Country Girl. Mousehole is a tiny village in Cornwall, England. You may be familiar with it. They filmed an American movie there called The English Gentleman, with Renay Zimmer and Guy Grant."

Excitedly, Amber exclaimed, "Oh, I loved that movie!"

Pleased, Devon continued, "Actually, it's because of that movie, or rather due to my working at the pub, Renay and Guy frequented, that I ended up in L.A."

Unable to control herself any longer, Amber squealed, "You met Renay Zimmer and Guy Grant! Oh my Lordy, I would just faint, if I met them."

Devon grinned slowly and said, "Well, if you think you could refrain from passing out, I would be happy to introduce you to them…"

He barely finished his sentence before Amber jumped out of her chair and ran over to Devon, grabbed his arm, and asked, "You know them personally? Like, you're friends with them?"

Devon stood, trying to pry Ambers death grip off his arm before he answered her, because once she heard his response, she was sure to do damage. "Um, well, if you promise not to tear my limb off, I'll tell you."

Amber looked down at her hands and said, "Oh, I'm so sorry, Devon."

She let go.

Devon rubbed his arm, backed up a few steps from Amber, and continued, "Yes, I know them both very well. Renay was kind enough to put me up when I arrived in L.A., and Guy and I are mates. We sail together whenever we are both in town. So when we get off this bloody island, I will throw a shin ding and you can chat them up."

Amber had to sit down before she fell down. At a loss for words, all she could manage was, "Wow."

Leanne, sitting back watching Devon and Amber, smiled and said, "Brit, I think you just made her day, or year, for that matter."

Devon undid his apron and said to the hens, "I cooked, you clean. Leonard, my boy, come with me."

* * *

An hour later, after the kitchen was cleaned, and everyone was dressed, they met up in the back yard. Rosalie took one look at all of the crap lying on the grass and said, "What the devil is all this?"

Devon stood and proudly said, "That, Pill Popper, is going to get us some of the best seafood straight out of the Puget Sound."

Confused, Rosalie said, "Huh?"

Leanne stepped over and picked up what looked like a rake and asked, "Where did you find all of this?"

Picking up a contraption that looked like a cage, Devon replied, "It was buried in the garage."

Amber walked over to the pile and picked up a pair of tall rubber boots, and said nostalgically, "These look like the slogging boots I used to wear when I went into the pen to feed the pigs."

Leonard, seeing her start to tear up, went over to her, and laid a hand on her shoulder and said, "You miss your family and the farm, don't you?"

Amber put down the boots and nodded, "Yes."

As not to lose his momentum, Devon spoke up, "Well, then, Little Miss Slogger, you will have some fun clamming, won't you? Boy Wonder, here, tells me that he spent many summers at his grand's house on an island not far from here, so he is familiar with the waters. Okay, let's go, everyone. Grab something…"

Before he could finish his sentence, Rosalie spoke, "Wait just one minute. You mean to tell me that we are going to schlep all the way back to the place where we were dumped off, and then go into that ice cold water hunting for shellfish? Do these shoes look like they can clump through the forest and go into the water?"

All at once, everyone looked down at Rosalie's two-hundred-dollar wedge sandals.

Leanne said to Rosalie, "What size shoe do you wear?"

"Size seven, why?" asked Rosalie.

Leanne took off running, yelling over her shoulder, "Hold on, I'll be right back."

With that said, she dashed into the house. She came back out a few minutes later carrying a ratty pair of sneakers and held them out to Rosalie, "Here, you can wear these."

Dumbfounded, Rosalie looked at the sneakers and said, "You've got to be kidding me."

"Well," said Leanne, "It's these, the ones you're wearing, or barefoot. Your choice?"

With that said, Rosalie grabbed them out of Leanne's hand, and mumbled, "Oh for Christ sake."

She proceeded to slip them on.

It took them 20 minutes to get to the beach and another ten to find a small, shallow cove; perfect for crabbing, and clamming. Devon, being the leader of the pack, doled out assignments, "Okay, Leanne, you can start raking over there. Rosalie," he said, as he handed her a pair of rubber gloves, "You head over to those rocks and look for mussels, and Amber, you put on those slogging boots, head out there, and look for...what are they called again, Boy Wonder?"

Leonard, untangling the fishing net, looked up, and said, "Crayfish."

Amber squealed so loud that Devon jumped back, tripped over Leonard, and ended up tangled in the fishing net.

"What the bloody hell," said a startled Devon, "What are you screeching about?"

Amber talking, a million miles a minute, said, "When I was a little girl, my granddaddy use to load us all up in the back of his pickup truck and drive us to Louisiana to go crawfishing. They're like itsy bitsy, teeny tiny lobsters. We set up a camp fire and granddaddy would boil them up with corn and potatoes. You just grab em' and snap their little heads off and dip them in sweet butter."

Devon, struggling to untangle himself from the net, said, "Swell. Then, why don't you head on out there and find us some."

With that said, and finally getting free of the net, he looked over at Leanne and Rosalie, only to find them doubled over, laughing. He brushed the sand off and grumbled, "Bloody hell," which made them laugh even harder.

They spent most of the day on the beach. When they were finally done, they packed up their haul of mussels, razor clams, crayfish, and oysters and headed back to the cabin with Devon and Leanne bringing up the rear.

Devon looked at Leanne and asked, "So, Queen Bee, what do you have in mind for our catch of the day?"

Leanne, deep in thought, didn't reply. Devon nudged her and said, "Earth to Leanne."

Snapping out of it, shaking her head, she said, "Sorry, I was kind of out there for a minute."

Eyeing her suspiciously, Devon inquired, "What has your mind all gaggled up?"

Leanne laughed and replied," Gaggled up, Rock Star? Is that British for occupied?"

Devon adjusted the sack on his shoulder and replied, "Well, yes, you were deep in thought. Want to share?"

Leanne was going to keep her thoughts to herself, but then decided bouncing them off Devon wouldn't be such a bad idea. "I didn't want to bring this up yet, but I'm starting to get a little concerned with the fact that the nut case life coaches haven't returned. Something's off and I can't quite put my finger on it."

Considering what Leanne said, Devon replied, "Well, it's crossed my mind, also. But I figured we'd wait and see if Chet shows up on Saturday and we ask him. Sound like a plan?"

Leanne nodded, "That was my thought too."

They were almost to the cabin, so Devon asked Leanne again, "Tell me, Chef Queen Bee, what have you in mind for the stuff in this sack?"

Leanne turned and looked at him, smiled mischievously, and said, "You'll have to wait and see."

Chapter 17

By the time they got back to the cabin, it was close to three. Amber, Devon, and Leonard took the rakes, cages, and nets to the side of the house to wash them down. Leanne brought their bounty of shellfish into the kitchen and dumped them into the sink. Rosalie was sitting at the kitchen table rubbing her throbbing leg. Leanne glanced over at her, and asked, "Is your leg aching?"

Rosalie looked up at her and replied, "Some. I guess I over did it today."

She went back to rubbing her leg.

Leanne smiled and replied, "Well, you could take Devon up on his offer to massage it for you."

Rosalie laughed and said, "I am not letting that Horn Dog touch me, even though he is hotter than a white hot poker."

Leanne put down the clams she was cleaning and left the room. She came back a few minutes later and handed Rosalie three little orange pills. Rosalie looked up at her with questioning eyes. Seeing the look, Leanne said, "Don't worry. They're just over the counter pain relievers."

She walked over to the fridge, took out the pitcher of tea, got two glasses from the cabinet, and sat down across from Rosalie. She poured them each a glass and pushed one over to Rosalie.

Picking up the tea and swallowing the pills, Rosalie turned to Leanne and said, "Thanks. Can I ask you a question?"

Leanne drank deeply from her glass and nodded.

Rosalie asked, "Why are you here?"

Leanne sat quiet for a minute, twisting the napkin in her hand, and then responded, "Honestly, I'm not sure. I pretty much told you everything the day Amber called for the meeting at the picnic table." Leanne sat forward and added,

"Except…for one thing that keeps poking at me, and I don't know why."

Rosalie eyed her and asked, "And what might that be, Locomotive?

Leanne stared across the table at Rosalie with a confused look on her face and replied, "Blake's a lawyer; a good negotiator. But there was no discussion. He just came home that night with the Claine Enlightenment Retreat brochure, plopped it on the table, and said three words, "Think about it," and left the room. Basically, he gave me an ultimatum, without giving me an ultimatum, if you know what I mean."

Rosalie sat forward and said, "That's what I'm talking about. Don't you think you could have worked things out with Blake through couples counseling? Why would you come to some island enlightenment retreat by yourself, when the problem concerns both you and Blake?"

Leanne took a sip of her ice tea, put the glass down, sat back, and sighed heavily, "I have been asking myself that question a lot lately, and I keep coming up with the same answer. I needed to find myself, before I can fix my marriage and whatever issues there are. I have my list but the numerous times I have approached Blake about them, he brushes them off, telling me I am over dramatizing again. I guess I'm hoping that coming here, and stepping out of my everyday life will give me some better prospective."

Rosalie nodded and said quietly, "I get it."

Just then, the back door banged open and Leonard, Amber, and Devon came in soaking wet and laughing. Rosalie and Leanne looked at them and shook their heads. Leanne got up and went back to the sink. Rosalie asked the soaking wet trio, "What have you children been up to?"

Devon grabbed three glasses form the cabinet and poured some tea and replied, "Oh just a little school yard fun."

That set the trio off again.

Leanne looked over her shoulder and said, "Well, do you think you could take your soaking wet asses out of the kitchen and let me get started on dinner?"

The three of them looked down at the puddles they were making on the floor.

Amber apologized, "Sorry, Leanne. I'll get some towels and then I'm going to take a nice hot shower."

Devon and Leonard looked at Leanne and both said at the same time, "What's for dinner?"

Leanne, having finished cleaning the shellfish, said, "You'll find out when I put it on the table. Now, shoo."

The school boys left the kitchen.

Rosalie turned to Leanne and said, "What can I do to help?"

Leanne, scurrying around the kitchen grabbing pots, and pans, said kindly, "Nothing. Why don't you get off that leg for a while?"

With that said, Rosalie headed for her bedroom.

A few hours later, once Leanne had everything simmering, she decided to run upstairs, and take a quick shower. Passing through the living room, she saw the gang. Amber and Leonard were on the couch talking, Rosalie was playing solitaire and Devon was building a fire.

She smiled and said to the group, "I'm going to take a quick shower. Dinner will be ready at seven, and no peeking. Devon, could I speak to you for a minute upstairs?"

All eyes shot to her like arrows. Flustered, she said, "Oh for Christ sake, get your minds out of the gutter."

She started up the stairs. They all turned to Devon, who shrugged, raised an eyebrow, and followed after Leanne.

Twenty minutes later, Leanne came back downstairs, walked past a smirking Rosalie, Leonard, and Amber and continued into the kitchen. She stopped dead in her tracks and said to a smiling Devon, "Wow...this looks great!"

Pleased with himself, Devon replied, "You are a mystery, Queen Bee."

After a few finishing touches, Leanne called the gang to dinner. Rosalie walked in first and surveyed the kitchen, looked over at Leanne and Devon, and said, "Well, aren't you full of surprises."

Leonard and Amber came in next. Amber's hands flew to her mouth. Speechless for the moment, Leonard guided her to the table with his smile on high beam. Amber trying to compose herself said, "You did this all for me?"

Tears were streaking down her face.

Leanne, trying not to cry herself, said, "Well, Country Bumpkin, there's nothing like a good ole' crawfish boil."

Arranging themselves around the simulated campfire, they dug into clams, mussels, oysters, crayfish, boiled potatoes, and corn on the cob, which was a gift from the Heavens above when Leanne went rummaging through the box freezer.

Chapter 18

Saturday brought with it a special gift, besides Chet's pending arrival with a food delivery; Sunshine! The past seven days were wet and gloomy, which seemed to match the moods of the five inhabitants of Claine Cabin.

Leanne was the first one awake and began her ritual, which she now likes to think of as her therapy, of making breakfast. However, being that their supplies were just about out, she didn't have many options. All she could rustle up was cereal, yogurt with berries, and left over bread for toast. As she was mixing the berries and yogurt, Rosalie walked into the kitchen, and proclaimed, "Hallelujah, Praise the Lord, is that really sunshine or am I still dreaming?"

Amused, Leanne said, "Nope, you're wide awake and yes, the sun is shining."

Rosalie poured herself a cup of coffee and sat down at the table. Leanne poured herself another cup and joined her. They both just sat there quietly staring out at the morning sun, until Amber walked in and said brightly, "Well, good morning, ya'll. And hello, Mr. Sunshine! Honestly, if we had one more day of rain, I was going to make a serious attempt to swim to civilization."

On that note, Devon stumbled into the kitchen, grunted, and went straight to the coffee pot. Leonard surprised everyone by walking in the back door carrying a bouquet of wild flowers. He proceeded to hand Amber a daisy, and then held out the rest to Leanne. Stunned, but touched, Leanne whispered, "For me?"

Leonard, feeling a little awkward, shuffled from foot to foot, said, "Well, um, I woke up early this morning and decided to go for a walk when I saw these wild flowers. I, um, well, wanted to say thank you for all that you do." Blushing, he abruptly turned, and sat down next to Amber.

Leanne, having difficulty finding her words hidden behind her tears, rose from the table, and went into the pantry. The others watched her go in and waited curiously for her to come out. After five minutes, Rosalie said, "Do you think one of us should go in there after her?"

Nobody responded because two seconds later Leanne emerged from the closet carrying a vase and a roll of paper towel. She went to the sink, filled the vase with water and arranged the flowers in it, walked over to the table, and placed the vase in the center.

She turned to Leonard and said, "Thank you. That was very thoughtful of you."

Devon, having watched all of this unfold, piped in, "Well, I guess someone has been working on her Bitch-o-Meter."

The table erupted in laughter.

As they finished up breakfast, Amber cheerfully said, "Well, ya'll, I, for one, know I'm sure ready to see Chet. Why don't we all get dressed and head to the beach to wait for him and Sadie?"

Devon picked up the dishes and headed for the sink. Smirking, replied to Leanne, "I think that's a novel idea."

It took Leanne about 20 seconds to make the connection, and then with humor in her voice, said, "Oh, no, you didn't."

Smiling cheekily at her, he responded, "Oh, yes, I did."

The other three were looking at them like they just landed from Mars.

Rosalie, not liking being left out of inside jokes, said, "What the hell are you two talking about?"

Feeling playful, Leanne responded, "Looks like Horn Dog here got his horny hands on my *Sixty Sides of Gray* novel."

Confused, Amber said, "Is that the book about kinky sex and..." then the light bulb turned on. "Oh, my Lord, Devon, I don't think that was a good idea." With that said, the room exploded with laughter.

Chapter 19

"I have to say, this feels glorious!" exclaimed Rosalie, leaning against a rock soaking up the sun.

Leanne, laying close by on a blanket reading, replied, "Amen to that sister."

Amber and Leonard had strolled off down the beach. Devon was sitting atop the rock, that Rosalie was leaning against, humming softly.

Rosalie looked up and said, "Hey, Rock Star. Can you put words to your humming?"

Devon tossed another pebble into the water and said, "Eventually."

He looked right at Leanne.

15 minutes later, they heard Amber and Leonard shouting, "The plane, the plane."

They shouted like the little guy from that television show about an island.

Devon jumped off the rock. Leanne and Rosalie looked up, shading their eyes from the sun. A few minutes later, they spotted the plane and watched as Chet laid Sadie down smoothly in the water. They all hurried to the dock to greet Chet. Once he shut down the engines and climbed out of the plane, Amber ran to him, and threw her arms around his neck, "Woo wee, am I happy to see you!"

Chet, trying to steady himself, said, "Well, I'd say so, Little Miss."

As the others made their way down the dock, Chet turned to Amber and said, "Young Lady, you are looking fit as a fiddle. Glad to see some meat on your bones and a smile on your pretty, country, girl face."

Amber blushed and said, "Well, Leanne turned out to be a real good cook; and between you and me, I am happy."

Leonard put his arm around her.

Chet smiled and nodded approvingly. Just then, the others reached the end of the dock. Devon greeted him with a, "Hello, mate," and a hand shake.

Leanne and Rosalie both greeted him cheerfully, with Leanne adding, "Wow, am I glad to see you."

Chet stepped back and gave the five inhabitants a once over and said, "Now, here, are you the same five grumpy," and turning to Amber, "And frightened lot that I dropped on this, here, island a month ago?"

Rosalie responded, "I believe so, Chet."

"Well," he said, "I can see those Claine folks work some magic."

Dead silence, then Rosalie replied, "Speaking of the magicians, they seemed to have disappeared. Do you happen to know where they might be?"

Looking confused, Chet rubbed his chin and said, "Nope. They don't contact me unless they need me to fly a group out here."

Feeling her antennae go up, Leanne asked, "You mean to tell me, that you don't fly them back and forth when they come to the island?"

Chet, starting to feel uncomfortable, replied, "That's right. They always say they have another way to get here. Maybe you should ask them when they come to visit next."

Leanne was starting to feel her Bitch-O-Meter climbing upwards. She took a deep breath, and before she could speak, Amber piped in, "Mr. Chet, we haven't seen Micah or Blair but once, since we got here. And let me tell you, that didn't go so well."

Chet, not liking what he was hearing, said, "Well, that don't seem right."

Before the group could begin a mutiny, Devon stepped in and said, "Chet, do you have any way to contact them?"

Chet rubbed his chin again and said, "No, Sir. When they need me, they call me on the telephone; tell me when and where, and I do it."

The five looked at each other, and then Leanne noticing Chet's concern, said, "Okay, well, if you do hear from them, would you pass on a message from us?"

Chet, feeling a little uneasy, said, "Um, well, I guess I could do that. What you want me to say?"

Leanne smiled and said, "Please tell them to get their phony asses to this island, pronto."

Chet, looking like he was ready to run for cover, said, "I'll pass it on for sure, if I hear from them."

With that said, Chet turned to Sadie, and started unloading the sacks of food.

Feeling guilty for speaking to Chet the way she did, Leanne told the others to start back, and she would catch up to them. Leanne turned to Chet; as he was about to board Sadie and yelled out, "Chet, hold on a minute."

She walked up to him and said, "I'm sorry I spoke to you that way. You are an innocent bystander in this whole mess."

Chet rubbed his chin, then looking at Leanne, he said, "Well, truth be told, I'm not liking what I'm hearing; those Claines leaving you on this island, and all."

Leanne kindly asked Chet, "Since you flew all this way to bring us supplies, would you like to come have lunch with us?"

Chet shook his head and replied, "That's right nice of you, but I've been gone all morning, so I need to be getting back."

Leanne, seeing sadness in his eyes; cautiously said, "Your wife must worry about you when you do these trips."

Chet looked out towards the water and said, "My Annie passed on some years back, but I have a couple of fur babies at home that need tending to."

Unsure what he was talking about, Leanne questioned, "Fur babies?"

Chet let out a rare laugh and said, "Bella and Blaze, my hunting hounds. They all I got now."

Leanne couldn't stop herself. She stepped over to Chet and wrapped her arms around him, and whispered, "Well, if you get lonely, you come back, and have a meal with us. And, bring Bella and Blaze with you."

Chet stepped back and tipped his cap to Leanne, and said, "Thank you kindly, ma'am."

As he boarded Sadie, Leanne yelled out, "Its Leanne, my name is Leanne."

They both smiled.

Chapter 20

After another five days of rain, the clan finally woke up to a spectacular sunny Thursday. They decided, after being cooped up for a week that they would head to the beach and have a picnic lunch. Leanne made sandwiches of leftover chicken, tomatoes, and fresh basil on her now famous focaccia bread. Leonard had gone out earlier and picked fresh berries, so Leanne drizzled a little balsamic on them, and added chopped fresh mint. Devon, being the forager of the garage, came up with a cooler. They loaded it with bottled waters, sandwiches, fruit, and set off.

Rosalie was in a mood and a half, and griped all the way to the beach. Once they spread the blanket, Leonard and Amber announced they were going to take a walk.

Being in a bitch mood, Rosalie snapped, "What the heck is going on with those two? They're like Beauty and the Geek."

Leanne looked at her and said sympathetically, "Why don't you go sit on that rock over there and soak your leg? I think the cold water will help with the ache."

Not having a witty comeback, Rosalie grumbled, and walked toward the water.

That left Devon and Leanne alone. Leanne sat down on the blanket and pulled her novel out of her bag. Devon plopped down next to her and grabbed the book out of her hand, and said, "How do you read this rubbish?"

Raising an eyebrow and quickly snatching the book back, she countered, "You tell me?"

Figuring his odds of an equally pliable retort, he surrendered with, "Touché."

Leanne adjusted herself on the blanket and asked Devon, "What are the odds that the Prom King and Queen will return?"

Feeling cheeky, he said, "Maybe that's a question for Boy Wonder."

Leanne looked at him and said, "Very funny, Romeo, but seriously, do you think they will show up again?"

Devon tossed the shell in his hand toward the water and replied, "Actually, I have been giving this a lot of consideration, and if I had to place a wager on it, I would say, yes, and soon."

Leanne, feeling cheeky herself, said, "Okay, Romeo, ten bucks says you're wrong. My take on it is they can't handle us. We're not like any of the others they have been hired to enlighten. I felt that way from the minute Rosalie tackled Red. They don't like to get their hands dirty; so when they encounter mud, they wash their hands of it, so to speak."

Devon gazed at her and said with a slow smile, "You're on, Queen Bee."

An hour later, the group was gathered on the blanket eating the picnic, when Rosalie, who was feeling better, said, "As I was soaking my leg, I had some time to think about how I would survive another seven weeks on this island."

Devon, with his mouth full, said, "And what did you come up with, Pill Popper?"

Rosalie stuck her tongue out at him and said, "Fun."

The other four looked at her like she had just downed a bottle of Oxycodone.

Amber, who hadn't said much during lunch, wiped her mouth, and said, "I'm game. And to be truthful with ya'll, I have not felt this free in a long time."

Devon blurted out, "Free? Bloody hell! We're being held captive on a deserted island!"

Amber, ever the optimist, said, "I know, I know. What I mean is, back in L.A., I was always trying to be someone I'm not. And back in Oklahoma, I couldn't wait to be someone else. What I'm saying is, being here with you guys has made me realize who I am."

And with that said, she grabbed Leonard by his cheeks, and kissed him full on the mouth.

Rosalie and Leanne shot a look at each other that said, "What the fuck?"

Devon casually said, "I would be up for a bit of fun."

Looking directly at Leanne, "Is that what you had in mind, Pill Popper?"

Still stunned, Rosalie replied, "Not exactly."

Leanne had to bring this to a halt, pronto. Her insides were on fire; between the damn book and Romeo's glares she was ready to self-combust. She took a sip of her water and turned to Rosalie and asked, "What did you have in mind?"

Rosalie, recovered enough to explain, said, "Okay, you know the chore chart, right? Well, what I was thinking was, the gurus put on there to paint the house, so that means there has to be paint somewhere."

Leanne, Leonard, and Amber not quite catching on, said, "Probably."

Devon on the other hand, caught on very quickly, and said, "Well, actually, I just happened to find a few cans of white paint, as I was rummaging around in the garage."

Rosalie smiled like the cat that ate the canary and said, "Perfect. Okay, so what I was thinking was what if we all painted what we are feeling on the house. So, if by some alignment of the stars, the gurus happen to show up, they'll see exactly how we are feeling."

Devon looked at Rosalie and smiled wickedly and said, "That is brilliant, Pill Popper."

Leanne, having jumped on the band wagon, so to speak, said, "Yes! We could also draw a symbol, of sorts, that brought us here. Maybe a wine glass for me," and looking at Rosalie she added, "Maybe a statue of the Virgin Mary for you?"

Then, Amber eagerly added, "I could make the Hollywood sign. You know; the one up on the hill?"

Leonard followed suit, literally, "I can make a deck of cards and some dice!"

The excitement was contagious until they all looked at Devon. Rosalie slapped her thigh, and said, "Romeo, can draw his willy!"

That just did them in. Leanne laughing tears, croaked, "Yeah, he can name it Dick."

Everyone but Devon was busting a gut. Once they regained their composure, Devon spoke, "Oh, aren't you all so clever." Then, looking straight at Leanne, said, "I'm game."

They packed up their picnic and headed back to the cabin, laughing, and chatting the whole way.

Chapter 21

After hearing Rosalie's crazy idea yesterday, they awoke Friday morning eager to start. Leanne fixed them all a hardy breakfast of scrambled eggs, bacon, toast, and of course, fresh berries. Devon got a pass on cleaning up after breakfast, since he spent time digging out the paint and supplies.

They were blessed with another beautiful mid-May morning. Amber and Leonard had been secretive and whispering all morning, so when they were ready to start, Amber said excitedly, "Well, ya'll, when I was growing up on the farm, I always dreamed of being a fashion model or movie star, so my momma would give me old white sheets to make dresses out of. One day, while wearing one of my many creations, Momma took us blueberry picking. We spent hours out in the bramble and because I hated the way they turned my fingers blue, I kept wiping my fingers on my fancy white dress. Lordy, I cried for a week straight because Momma couldn't get the stains out. Anyway, that got me to thinking; since we only have white paint, I thought it would be really fun to add some blueberries to the white paint and make it blue. And, I saw some dandelions and I remembered how they always turned my fingers yellow, too."

Rosalie stood and said, "That is a great idea, Country Girl. Hang on, I'll be right back."

Rosalie ran into the house. Five minutes later, she came back out carrying what looked like a small suitcase. She proceeded to lay it down on the picnic table and unzipped the sides.

The minute she flipped it open, Amber squealed like a stuck pig, "Rosalie, you are so smart! But my goodness gracious, do you always lug around a hundred bottles of nail polish?"

Rosalie, pleased with herself, said, "Well, you never know what color a girls going to be in the mood for. So, I bring every color of the rainbow, plus some."

Thrilled, Amber said, "Well, I'd say so, and honestly Rosalie, this is just perfect. Thank you so much!"

Rosalie patted Amber's hand, clutching a devil red nail polish, and said, "No, Country Girl, this was your idea."

Everyone gathered around the table and chose a color of nail polish to add to their plastic container of white paint. Once everyone had their custom color ready, Devon spoke up and said, "Pill Popper, since this was your idea, I think it is only appropriate that you get to write the first word. So, have at it, Pippa."

The others concurred, so Rosalie picked up her cup of custom colored paint, walked to the house, and wrote her word. She finished and turned to the group and said, "That one's for Blair."

They all read 'bitch' in bright red letters.

They spent Friday and Saturday painting their feelings on Claine Cabin. When they finally finished, they stepped back, and assessed their work. Devon was the first to speak, "That looks bloody marvelous. I think we have made our feelings known."

The group walked around the house in silence, reading all the colorful words. It looked like a rainbow dictionary: angry, sad, depressed, lonely, ugly, pain, friends, family, wine, women, divorce, homesick, geek and so on.

They sat down at the picnic table and stared at the house in silence. Finally, Leanne stood and said, "I don't know about you guys, but I'm starving."

The others agreed. They began cleaning up the paint cups and brushes. Devon walked over and took a paint brush from Leanne's hand, and said, "We've got this, Queen Bee. Why don't you go get washed up and start dinner?"

She smiled thankfully and said, "That sounds like a plan."

* * *

After finishing off a delicious dinner of pasta with a fresh tomato basil sauce and two loaves of Leanne's famous focaccia bread, Rosalie pushed her plate away and said, "That was delicious. The only thing missing was a good bottle of Red."

The room went silent and all eyes darted to Leanne.

Oblivious to why they were all quiet as a church mouse, Leanne said, "What?"

Rosalie, looked at the others, and repeated Leanne's question, "What?

Leanne finally caught on and said, "Okay, listen here, all of you, I've told you my story. I am not on this God forsaken island to find the path to sobriety. I have life issues I need to work out, regarding my health and happiness. And as I told you, Blake suggested, his word, not mine, that I take this enlightenment retreat journey. And truth be told, when I saw that brochure with the gorgeous house, the pool, and spa, the meditation rooms, and everything else it offered, I thought, 'hell, this may be the answer the stars couldn't give me'."

With that laid out on the table, she turned to Rosalie and said, "I agree with you. A nice bottle of Red would have complimented this meal perfectly."

The silence lingered a few seconds more until Amber spoke up, "Leanne, when I first met you, I was quite honestly scared to the bone of you. You were like a Mack truck ready to run over anything that got in your way. As my Daddy would say to Momma, "Your stink eye could burn down the barn." But when I was down and out, you picked me back up. So don't you ever question your goodness; it's pure and real, like you."

Leanne, taken back by Amber's kind words, reached over and held her hand, and said, "Thank you, Amber."

Leonard, having been the quietest of the group, said, "Can I say something?"

All heads turned to him and nodded.

"Um, well, it's about this island being miserable and all. Since I've been here and met all of you, I can't help but to think how lucky I am. I'm a 25-year-old geek who still lives with his parents, works for his parents, has no say in said parents multi mega million dollar company, has no friends except the one's that used me for my illegal casino, and, the worst of it is, I'm still a virgin!"

Leonard's thick black bottle lens glasses slid down his nose and fell onto the table. He blinked back tears and put his face in his hands. The other four stared in stunned silence with wide eyes and open mouths.

Amber, sitting next to Leonard, reached over, and grabbed his hands. Leonard was mortified and would not let go of his face. Amber soothingly said, "Leonard...Leonard, look at me."

Slowly he spread his fingers, and peeked out at her.

"Leonard, look all the way at me."

He did as she asked, if ever so slowly. Once he was looking at her, she said, "Leonard, you are one of the kindest, sweetest, smartest men I have ever met. If it wasn't for you and all of your compassion, I would have curled up in a ball until these 12 weeks were over. But you walked with me, you talked to me, and, most importantly, you listened to me, so I want you to hear me now; I am your friend, I want to be your girlfriend, and, um, well I'm still a virgin, too, and plan on staying that way, until I get married."

Now Leonard joined Rosalie, Leanne, and Devon and stared wide eyed and mouth open at her.

Rosalie, not able to keep quiet a minute longer, said, "Oh, this is priceless."

She turned to Devon and said, "Hey, Romeo, you might need a cold shower after this."

This sent her into a bout of laughter.

Leanne, hanging on by a thread, said, "Stop it, Rosalie," but the dam broke and the two hens had their heads on the table, shoulders bouncing with laughter.

Devon, not amused, said, "Well, aren't you two quite the pair of giggling hens."

This brought down the room.

Composing herself, Leanne stood, picked up her plate, and put it in the sink. Devon, eyeing her, said, "I've got it, Cackling Hen."

Leanne cleared her throat and said, "Okay, just put them in the sink for now. We'll have dessert first."

Leanne went into the pantry and brought out a wild berry crumble, which had been cooling. Devon grabbed five plates and forks, and followed her to the table. Leanne spooned out the crumble onto the plates and passed them around.

After taking his first bite, Devon looked directly at Leanne, and said, "Queen Bee, I don't know how I will survive when we get off this bloody island, without your berry desserts."

Rosalie, as always, on top of her game, said, "Hmmm, you're going to miss her berry desserts, are you?"

Leanne, diverting her eyes from the others, kept her head down, and continued to eat.

Devon, taking advantage of where this conversation was going, mumbled, "Among other things."

Sweet Jesus, thought Leanne, *I'm going to need a cold shower.*

Chapter 22

The Claine Cabin inhabitants woke to a glorious Sunday morning. Leanne was in the kitchen, preparing breakfast. She woke early, wanting to try a recipe she thought of during the night for berry scones. She stirred the batter, humming happily to herself.

Not hearing Devon walk into the kitchen behind her, she was startled half to death when he said, "Can you put words to that humming, Queen Bee?"

Leanne whipped around and said, "What the hell! Why are you sneaking around the kitchen?"

Devon, amused, reached out, and gently wiped away the batter that got flung onto Leanne's face. Feeling like she got zapped by the toaster, Leanne backed up, and Devon moved forward, occupying the inch or so between them. Devon replied quietly, "You were lost in thought, humming, and I wanted to listen for a minute before interrupting. What song was that?"

Leanne, feeling very flustered, backed up another inch, and turned toward the sink. With her back to Devon, she said, "It's nothing. Just a lull-a-bye I sing to the twins at bedtime."

Devon walked over to the coffee pot and poured himself a cup. Holding out the pot, he asked Leanne, "Do you want a cup?"

Moving back to her batter, she replied, "No, thank you. Since you nearly scared the heart out of me, I think I'll pass."

Devon replaced the pot and moved closer to Leanne, "What are you working on, Chef?"

Leanne, trying to put a little distance between them, went to the refrigerator to get the berries, and answered, "Scones."

Devon arched an eyebrow and said, "Really? Scones happen to be one of my favorites, being British and all."

Returning with the berries, Leanne gently folded them into the batter, and casually said, "Well, don't get too excited, Romeo. This is my first attempt at making them, so they may not be anything like your British scones."

Devon moved in a little closer, peeking over Leanne's shoulder and replied seductively, "Oh, I'm sure your scones will be fabulous, Queen Bee."

Oh boy, thought Leanne, as Devon breathed on her neck. She needed to put an end to this. Turning toward Devon, she put a hand on his bare chest and gently pushed him away, and said, "Well, we'll never know, if you don't let me get them into the oven, will we?"

And just at that moment, with Leanne's hand on Devon's bare chest, Rosalie walked into the kitchen.

Never at a loss for words, Rosalie stopped dead in her tracks, and stared wide eyed at the scene in front of her. Recovering quickly, she said, "Oh for Christ sake! What the hell is in the water in this place? First, Beauty and the Geek and now, Romeo and the Queen."

Leanne quickly put the scones in the oven, turned, and said, "It's not what you think, Rosalie. Devon was hovering over me and my scones. I was just pushing him away."

"Ha! I bet," said Rosalie as she poured herself a cup of coffee and sat down at the table.

Just then, Amber and Leonard came in the back door. Amber, looking like a beaming ray of sunshine, said, "Good morning, ya'll, what a beautiful morning it is. Leonard and I just took a walk on the beach. And let me tell you, there is nothing more eye-opening than a sunrise over the water."

Rosalie, not missing a beat, said, "I'm not so sure about that, Corn Flower. I had my eyes opened wide by just walking into the kitchen."

Flustered, Leanne busied herself getting the plates out of the cabinet, while a smirking Devon sat down at the table and said, "Well, nothing starts my day better than watching a beautiful woman whip up a batch of scones."

Having lost all control of the situation, Leanne headed for the pantry. Rosalie looked at the others and said with amusement, "And into the pantry, she goes again."

Leonard poured him and Amber a cup of coffee, and sat down at the table. He turned to Rosalie, and said, "What's going on? Is Leanne okay?"

Rosalie took a sip of her coffee and said, "Oh, I think she's just dandy."

Leanne emerged from the pantry carrying a basket for the scones. Avoiding any other innuendos from the group, she brightly said, "Found it."

Amber looked at her and said, "Leanne, are you alright? You're looking a little flushed."

Reaching for her cheek, Leanne quickly said, "Yes, I'm fine. It's just a little warm in here."

Rosalie scoffed and said, "Warm? Ha! I would say it's damn near blazing hot!"

Devon added, "Smoldering hot."

Leonard and Amber were completely lost. Looking at Devon and Rosalie, Amber asked, "Did we miss something?"

Just as Rosalie was going to reply, the oven timer dinged, and Leanne shouted, "Scones are done!"

Devon looked at her, smirked, and said, "Saved by the bell, Queen Bee."

* * *

After breakfast, the group decided to get their chores done early. Rosalie, being on laundry duty, said, "I'm going to wash the bed sheets today. So, if you could strip them off your bed and leave them in a pile, I'll come get them. Also, Horn Dog, do you know if there is any rope in the garage? The dryer has been acting up lately, so I thought maybe we could make a clothing line out back and air-dry the sheets."

Hearing this, Amber got all excited and said, "That's a great idea, Rosalie! Growing up on the farm, we never had a clothes dryer; just an old Maytag washing machine. So, Momma would hang everything on a rope tied to two trees. Hanging the laundry with my sister Hannah, was one of my favorite things to do. Momma would bring out a basket of wet sheets and towels and Hannah and I would pretend we were the house maids for a really rich family that lived in the castle.

We'd talk about our dreams of what we wanted to be when we grew up."

Caught up in Amber's story, Leanne asked, "How many siblings do you have?"

Amber happily answered, "Well, there's me. Hannah, who is two-years older than me. My brother B.J, being Bailey Junior after my Daddy, he's the oldest. My younger brother, Teddy, and the baby of the family is my brother, Petey."

"Wow, that's quite the clan," said Devon, "Where are they all now?"

Amber, feeling nostalgic, replied, "Well, it's been a while since I was last home. But we all talk on the phone at least once a week, so the latest news was: Hannah, who married her high school sweetheart, Clay Donovan, just had baby number four. She is over the moon to finally have a baby girl after three boys. Bailey is married to Jenna Wilkins, who is Hannah's best friend since they were three. They have two kids; Brandon and Betsy. They built a house on our land and Bailey works with Daddy on the farm. Teddy is in the Army, and is stationed in Germany. And Baby Petey is the star quarterback of Stillwater High School."

Trying to take all this information in, the clan just nodded. Rosalie, curious as a cat, said, "How did you end up in crazy L.A.?"

Amber giggled and said, "Well, like I told you, I was always wanting to be someone else growing up on the farm, not just a country girl with a pretty face and a Homecoming Queen crown. So, I sat Momma and Daddy down the day I graduated high school and said, "Momma, Daddy, I want to go to Hollywood and be a star. Well, let me tell you that went over like a fox in the hen house. Daddy said no right away. Momma, well, she just sat there wringing her hands not saying a word. And believe me, when Momma says nothing, so best, you."

Totally engrossed in Amber's story, Leanne asked, "How in the world did you convince them to say yes?"

Amber replied, "I didn't. Hannah did. She came over to the house the next morning to drop off Clay Jr., and Momma told her about it. Hannah, being one to always get her way, said, "Momma, you and Daddy knew this day was coming. Amber is destined for bright lights and big cities. You can't hold her back from trying. If she doesn't try, she will never be happy. Why don't you make a deal with her? Give her one year to spread her wings, and if it doesn't work out, you know she'll fly right back home." So, that night, Momma and Daddy sat me down and said that I could go on one condition, that if I ever felt lonely or scared, I was to turn around and come straight back home."

Amber felt her emotions start to surface, but continued, "So the next day, I packed my things. Daddy gave me five thousand dollars they had been saving up for my college education, and He and Bailey Jr. drove me straight through to L.A. I'll never forget the look on Daddy's face when he pulled up in front of the apartment I found on the internet. I thought he was going to put the truck in reverse and high tail it back to Oklahoma, with me in tow. But he didn't. He took a deep breath, got out of the truck, and said, "Okay, baby girl, go find those bright lights and let them know you have arrived."

Not able to hold back the tears, Amber picked up her napkin and wiped the tears away, and said, "At first, I was lost and scared. Then one day, I woke up, and I said to myself, "Well, Amber, it's time you go find those bright lights," so I went to a photographer to get some pictures taken, and that's when I met Giovanni. He took me under his wing right from the get go. He had a bunch of business connections which got me through some doors. I got some modeling jobs, about a dozen commercials, and one small part in a movie; but when I started hanging out with the pretty 'bad boys' and staying out until all hours of the night, things started to spiral downhill. Whenever I called home, I made sure the egg was sunny side up, if you know what I mean. But in all honesty, I was miserable and flat out exhausted. And, from what I saw in the mirror, I can see why Gio believed the rumors about me using cocaine. Yes, I tried it once. And right after, I sneezed, and blew it all off the table, which did not go over well with that crowd. From that point on, I just stayed away, while Joe went off with his friends."

Leanne reached over and took Ambers hand in hers, and said, "Honey, you said you called home once a week. Won't your parents be worried sick when they haven't heard from you in almost six weeks?"

Amber lowered her head and said quietly, "I told them I was going to Hawaii to shoot a movie for three months, and I wouldn't be able to call home. It would break their hearts, if they knew the truth."

Dissolving into tears, Amber laid her head on Leonard's shoulder, as he wrapped his arm around her.

Leanne said, "Amber, honey, I'm sure they'll understand. They love you and want to protect you. They will just be happy you came home."

Devon, having listened to Amber's story, decided it was time to lighten the mood and said, "Don't worry, Blondie. Once you bring Boy Wonder here home, they'll forget all about you being M.I.A."

Rosalie added, "That's right, Country Bumpkin. Once they get a load of your gazillionaire boyfriend, they'll be over the moon planning a big ole country, shindig of a wedding."

Amber lifted her head and looked at Leonard, who was looking a tad pale and said, "They're gonna just love you, like I do."

Amber kissed him on his cheek.

Leonard, nervous as a cat, said, "Well, I'm not sure they're going to be over the moon with their beautiful baby girl bringing home a gambling geek," which set the table into a fit of laughter.

Composing herself, Leanne said, "Okay, Gang, let's get our chores done, and tonight we'll have a backyard barbeque in honor of the happy couple. Devon, do you think you could make some kind of fire pit to grill the steaks on?"

Devon flashed a wicked grin at Leanne and said, "I believe I can do better than that, Queen Bee."

The group adjourned for the day to get on with their chores.

Chapter 23

Leanne finished mowing the lawn, and went inside to get some cold tea. She grabbed five glasses out of the cabinet, set them on a tray, grabbed the pitcher of ice tea from the refrigerator, and headed out back. Rosalie was hanging the last of the sheets on the makeshift clothes line that she and Amber rigged up. Amber was loading the vegetables, which she picked into a sack.

Leanne shouted out, "Time for a break. Come have a glass of cold tea."

Rosalie hung the last sheet on the line and walked over to the table, and said, "You don't have to ask me twice."

She proceeded to pick up a glass of tea and drain it straight to the bottom.

Amber plopped down on the bench and said, "Woo Wee, where did this heat come from? It feels like an August day in Oklahoma."

She drank her tea straight to the bottom like Rosalie.

Amused, Leanne said, "Honestly, I'm starting to lose track of the days. I can't believe it's the middle of May already and, nonetheless, five weeks have passed us by."

Rosalie, helping herself to another glass of tea, said, "Oh, don't you worry, Locomotive. I've been hash marking my prison cell since the day I got here, counting down until they spring me."

Leanne and Amber giggled.

Just then, they heard Leonard and Devon hootin' and hollerin' around the side of the house. Amber looked at Leanne and said, "What in the world? Those two have to be up to no good. I haven't seen hide or hair of them for hours."

Leanne stood and said, "Come on, girls. Let's go find out what all the fun is about."

All three women marched around to the corner of the house, and saw Devon and Leonard huddled over some kind of wooden table.

Amber put both hands on her hips and said, "What in the world are you two up to?"

Leonard ran over to Amber, picked her up, twirled her around, and said, "Come see."

The three hens walked over to where Devon was standing. He stepped aside and said, "Ta da, Cackling Hens! I give you the one and only, Leonard original, custom made, barbeque grill."

All three hens stared in amazement. Amber broke the trance when she squealed, "Leonard, did you make that?"

Feeling proud, he replied, "Yup, with help from Devon, of course."

Devon shot back, "Oh no, Boy Wonder. This was all you. I found the pieces, but you put the puzzle together."

Leanne stepped forward, circling the grill, "Wow," she said, "And are these the old wood pallets from the side of the garage?"

"Yup," said Devon, "And that there is an old copper sink I found buried in the garage."

Amber stepped closer and said, "You used chicken wire for the grate? I remember, as a kid on the farm, my brothers were always fighting about whose turn it was to fix the hen house. Nobody wanted to touch the chicken wire because it scratched them up."

Devon held out his scratched hands and said, "Oh yes, I can vouch for that. I found an old screen window and had a devil of a time getting the wire attached."

Rosalie stepped forward and ran her hand over the wooden surface, and said, "I guess you have some talents outside the bedroom, after all."

Devon stepped over to Rosalie, gave her a peck on the cheek, and replied, "And then some, Pill Popper."

He turned to Leanne, and asked, "So, Queen Bee, what do you think, will this do for barbequing those steaks?"

Still in awe, Leanne replied, "I'll say."

Amber turned to Leonard and gave him a big fat kiss on the lips and said, "Come around back and have a glass of cold tea.

You must be as thirsty as a drought stricken tree; you, too, Devon."

Leonard, still spinning from the kiss, said, "Okay, Devon, let's carry this around back and get the wood stacked in it."

The group headed to the backyard, got the grill set up, and gathered around the picnic table for some tea.

Leanne said to Leonard and Devon, "You guys did great. I'm going to head inside, get cleaned up, and start prepping dinner. Its 4:30 now. How does 6:30 sound for dinner? That way, you can get the grill going around 5:30. I'll need it really hot by six for the steaks."

Rosalie, having been uncharacteristically quiet, said, "Speaking of steak, something's been nagging at me and I can't quite get a grip on what it is. So, let me ask you guys. Does anyone else find it odd that we got red meat in this delivery? I mean when we arrived here, the house was fully stocked with more of a focus on vegetarian. Then, all of a sudden, this delivery is packed with meats, chips, and other goodies, for lack of a better word?"

Leanne, knowing exactly what Rosalie was talking about, said, "You know, I was thinking the same thing when I was unpacking the sacks that day. But I just figured that since the gurus washed their hands of us, they told Chet to do the shopping."

Devon sat up slowly and looking right past Leanne, said, "Well, that might not be entirely true. It looks like someone may want to play in the mud again."

Leanne, not quite sure what he meant, until she saw the look on Amber and Leonard's face, looked at Rosalie and together, very slowly, they turned around to see the gurus approaching from across the lawn.

Rosalie said, "Well, I'll be damned. Look what just climbed out from under a rock."

Devon got up and walked over to stand next to Leanne, and said to her, "Looks like you owe me ten dollars."

Amber and Leonard got up and joined Devon, Leanne, and Rosalie to form a united front. As the gurus approached, Blair yelled out, "Hello, hello. We are so happy to see you. We wanted to surprise you and come a little earlier."

Leanne, the Locomotive, started her engine, "Really? Is that so? I would say you are late, by like, four weeks!"

Rosalie eyeing the red headed matador and her puppet said, "Why are you two so tan?"

The puppet, Micah, responded cheerily, "We were in Hawaii…"

He didn't get the chance to finish his sentence because the matador pinched his arm and finished for him, "Yes, that's right. We had to tend to a very disturbing situation with one of our long time clients, an emergency of sorts."

The Locomotive took a step closer to the matador and said, "So, what you are saying is, you had a four week emergency with, most likely, a very rich client on a Hawaiian island and did not take into consideration that you abandoned five people on a Washington State island, who paid you handsomely for the privilege of seeing your fake ass faces just once!"

Micah looking a tad bit nervous, said, "No, no. We were only in Hawaii for two weeks and…"

Blair punched him in the arm and said, "Now let's not get all hot and bothered about this. What matters is we are here now. Oh, is that ice tea? We would love some. Why don't we take it inside and catch up, shall we?"

Leanne lurched forward, but Rosalie grabbed her arm and held her back, then she turned to Red, and said, "Yes, what a lovely idea, why don't we? After you."

Leanne shot daggers at Rosalie, but Rosalie just put a finger to her lips and smiled. It only took five seconds for the matador to implode. As Blair and Micah turned toward the house, having only taken a few steps, Blair stopped dead in her tracks, and screamed, "Oh my God! What have you done?"

Rosalie stepped forward and said, "Well, Red, you left us that chore list, which included painting the house, which we did. And since you asked us at our one and only enlightenment session to write down our feelings, we have. You know the saying, "Kill two birds with one stone," I think we accomplished that, don't you?"

Blair's face was the color of her hair. She was breathing so heavy; she looked like the big bad wolf getting ready to blow down the little piggy's house. She took a step closer to Rosalie, and screamed, "You are all fucking crazy! I want that vandalism off my house, now!"

Devon walked over and got between Blair and Rosalie and said, "That's not going to happen, Prom Queen. Though, what is going to happen is, you are going to answer some questions. Starting with where have you been and why has it taken you four weeks to show your face here again?"

Blair stepped back to Micah, thrust her chin upwards and said, "We don't have to answer any of your questions regarding our whereabouts."

The Locomotive moved into the fray and said, "Oh, I think you do. And what I would like to know is why hasn't Chet been transporting you back and forth to the island?"

Micah put his hands in his pockets and shuffled his feet looking like a boy who got caught stealing from the cookie jar. He looked at Blair and said, "Um, well, you see, it's not always convenient for Chet to come and get us. So, we, um, take our yacht. I mean boat."

Blair, glaring at him, said, "Shut the hell up!"

She turned to Leanne, poked her in the chest, and said, "You don't get to ask the questions, Miss Chardonnay. You answer ours."

Ut oh, that may not have been the wisest of the guru moves.

Leanne stepped forward into Blair's face and said, "Oh, you will answer our questions, even if I have to beat it out of you."

Just then, Micah grabbed Blair's arm and pulled her back a few feet. At the same time, Devon put a restraining arm around Leanne.

Leonard, having been behind them with Amber, said, "What I don't get Blair is why bring us out here at all, if you weren't planning on spending time with us?"

Blair flipped her hair back and said, "Figure it out, Einstein. You're a gambling man. You should know what drives a person."

Leonard eyed her and said, "It's the money. We're not people to you; we're a paycheck."

Blair smirked and said, "Oh, you are smarter than you look, nerd."

Well, that was another big ut oh. Without warning, Amber ran flying past the others and headed straight for Blair. And in a voice unbeknownst to the group, she growled, "What did you call him?"

Amber dove at Blair and caught her by her hair. From there, it was like two tumble weeds that had blown down a dirt road. Micah scrambled to get a grip on Blair, while Devon and Leonard both had to hold Amber back.

Blair, looking like she lost a dog fight, took off running for the woods with Micah close on her heels. She stopped just at the edge of the woods, and yelled, "You can all rot here for the next six weeks, because there is no way you are getting a refund."

They disappeared into the woods.

The clan re-grouped at the picnic table. Amber, still with a bee in her bonnet, said, "Who does she think she is? Calling Leonard a nerd."

Leonard took her hand and said, "Well, I kind of am."

Amber shot back, "No, you're not. You're a genius, and people who are dumb say mean things because they are jealous."

Leanne, having parked the Locomotive, said, "Well, if you ask me, those two just showed their true colors. They are frauds, like I have been saying all along."

Rosalie, having a chance to calm down, said, "Well, I think it's time we start thinking about a way off this hell hole of an island."

Leonard looked at Rosalie and replied, "That's what Amber and I have been doing for weeks now. We've walked up and down the beach for miles in both directions, and there isn't anything out there."

Devon, keeping his thoughts to himself for the time being, said, "Okay. Why don't we all get cleaned up and continue on with our plans for a barbeque? I, for one, am really looking forward to a hunk of beef."

Resigned, Leanne said, "Amber, Rosalie, I could use a hand in the kitchen. Let's get cleaned up and meet back in the kitchen in 30 minutes."

With that said, the hens headed into the house.

Chapter 24

An hour later, the kitchen was bustling. Amber was putting the finishing touches on the salad, Rosalie checked the potatoes in the oven, and Leanne was prepping the steaks for the grill.

Rosalie turned to Amber, and asked, "Hey, Country Girl. I was pretty impressed with your tackling skills, where did you learn that move?"

Amber washed her hands, picked up the dish towel, turned to Rosalie, and said, "Well, when you grow up in a house with brothers always picking on you, a girl's gotta defend herself. Hannah was always coming to my rescue when Bailey would start acting like a baboon. But one time when she wasn't around, Bailey took Miss Lily, my favorite doll. I got so angry I just went at him like a bull, head down and fast as lightening, and flattened him, but good. Daddy had to break it up and when he got us separated and found out that Bailey was being a butthead, he said, "Baby girl, you got to be mindful of other people. When they get to bullying you, you got every right to defend yourself. So, good for you on landing Bailey on his backside." From that day on, Bailey never messed with me again. And let me tell you, nobody is going to mess with my man."

Rosalie smiled and said, "Good for you, Country Bumpkin."

Leanne, listening to Rosalie and Amber, asked, "So, Amber, what do you think your momma and daddy are going to say when you bring Leonard home to meet them?"

Amber grinned from ear to ear and said, "Oh, Momma is just going to be over the moon. She always told me growing up, "Amber, you listen here, when you find Mr. Right, you make sure he treats you good and loves you for you, not what he wants you to be. And if you're lucky enough to find Prince

Charming, you hang on tight and love him with all your heart."
Well ya'll, Leonard is my Prince Charming and I'm hanging on
tight. Daddy, on the other hand; well, I'm his baby girl, so no
boy is ever going to be good enough for me. But I think he'll
take a liking to Leonard, because he's a good man and he treats
me right. However, I think with Leonard being a gazillionaire,
like Rosalie said, that may be a problem. We don't have much
money and Daddy was always griping to Momma about 'those
rich ranchers, always taking what's not theirs. Just because they
got the big dollars.'"

Leanne turned to Amber and said, "Honey, I think your
momma and daddy will love Leonard. They will see through
your eyes how happy he makes you."

Amber walked over and embraced the other two hens, and
said, "Thank you."

Just then, Devon and Leonard came in the back door,
Leonard excitedly said, "We've got the grill good and hot,
Leanne."

When he caught sight of the three hens huddled together, he
quickly said, "What's the matter, Amber? Are you okay?"

Amber smiled and said, "I'm more than okay, and I have
you to thank for that."

Dumbfounded, Leonard said, "Thank me for what?"

Amber giggled and said, "For being my Prince Charming."

Leonard, still baffled looked at Rosalie, who clarified for
him, "She's in love with you, Brainiac. You better do right by
her or you'll have me climbing up your back like a bad rash."

Leanne added, "Me, too."

Devon, coming to Leonard's rescue looked directly at
Leanne, and said, "I wouldn't mind you climbing up my back."

Rosalie, feeling like she was trapped on the love boat, said,
"Oh for Christ sake, can we just eat?"

And so, they did.

* * *

Devon finished off the last bite of his steak, pushed his
plate back, and announced, "That had to be one of the best
steaks I have ever had. And I have had my fair share all around
the world."

Leanne, feeling pleased, said, "I didn't do anything special to them; just a little salt, pepper, and rubbed garlic. But I have to agree, it was excellent."

Amber added, "Well if you ask me, I think what made them so good was the way they were cooked on Leonard's amazing grill."

Rosalie agreed and added nostalgically, "I think the burning wood added great flavor. I remember this restaurant Harold and I went to on our honeymoon in Tahiti. It was an open air shack on the beach. They built a fire pit in the sand, and kept adding wood to it. They cooked all the meat, fish, and vegetables on it, which were out of this world. They knew we were on our honeymoon, so they set up a table for two, down the beach by the water's edge. Lit candles and laid flower leis around our necks. One of the locals was playing a guitar, so Harold asked him if he knew a song called *Starry Nights*, which was our wedding song. He did, so Harold took my hand, and asked me if he could have this dance. We swayed to the music and the sound of the surf…"

Choking up, Rosalie stopped.

Amber, caught up in the moment, said, "That sounds so romantic."

Leanne, seeing the sadness in Rosalie's eyes, said quietly, "Tell us about Harold."

Rosalie cleared her throat and dabbed at her eyes, and finally said, "Ha! Harold. Well, let's see. I met him when I was 30. I had just started my own real estate company. I was in my office one day and in walked this short, bald, round man with a smile as wide as his face. He walked right up to me and said, "Hello, Little Lady. How are you this fine day?" I looked up at him, annoyed, and said, "Great. What can I do for you?" He said, "Well, I'm in the market for a house and seeing that you sell houses, I thought you might be able to help me." At this point, I am ready to pass him off to Denise, who had just started working for me, and honestly, I really didn't want to be bothered with this jolly fellow. So, I said, "Well, I'm quite busy, but I can have Denise help you." He sat right down in the chair in my office, and said, "Nope, that's okay. I have all the time in the world to wait for you to not be busy." Well, as you all have come to know, I don't have much patience for people, so I said to him, "Well then, I guess you'll be waiting a while," and he said, "Works for me. Just means I can sit here and take in your beauty." Figuring I wasn't going to be able to ditch him, I schedule some appointments to show him houses. We must have seen 50 houses and none of them 'tickled his belly' as he would say. After a month of this bullshit, I decided to shake him lose, so I said to Harold, "Okay, listen here, you Shyster. I have no time for your games. Either you're buying a house or you're not. Stop wasting my time." He laughed his deep rolling laugh and said, "Well, Rosalie, here's what I'm thinking. How about you and I have dinner tonight and tomorrow we'll go back out and find us a house?" I was exasperated and wanted nothing more than to be rid of him, I agreed purely on the fact that I would get a sale out of him, along with a big fat commission."

Amber, totally engrossed in Rosalie's story, asked, "Well did you, I mean go out to dinner with him and then sold him a house?"

Rosalie smiled, and responded, "Oh and then some. I married him a week later and he bought me my dream house."

Devon, amused by this rotund man, said, "So his intentions were never to buy a house. He was actually fancying you."

Rosalie laughed and said, "Apparently so. I'm a client at the Chiropractor office he owns, though, I never met him. I am a regular with Raul. But according to Harold, he fell in love with me the first time he saw me. He was terrified of me, go figure. So, he never approached me. Then one day Raul told him, and I quote, "Mr. Harold, put on your big girl panties and go get her," so, he did."

Amber sat back and said, "Wow! That is so sweet."

Rosalie sighed and said, "Yeah, well, sweet turned sour five years later. And now, we're divorced. End of story."

Leanne eyed Rosalie and said, "I don't think so. I think this story has another chapter."

Rosalie scoffed, "Nope. I have sworn off men. They are too much trouble. And frankly, I'm not in the market. One and done."

Leonard, having been quiet this whole time said, "Rosalie, don't take this the wrong way, but I know a bluff when I see one. I say you're still hooked on Harold."

The other three agreed.

Rosalie, not wanting to discuss this further, said, "Leanne, dinner was delicious. But I am exhausted, so I think I'll turn in early."

Leanne knew Rosalie needed some space so she said, "Sure, good night."

Rosalie stood and picked up her plate, but Devon put a hand on her arm and said, "I've got it, Pill Popper."

Rosalie looked around the table and said, "Good night."

Amber looked at Leonard and said, "Well, I'm as full as a momma cat carrying a litter. What do you say we go take a walk on the beach?"

Leonard looked at Leanne and Devon, and asked, "Can we help clean up before we go?"

Devon smiled and replied, "No, go on, Lover Boy. Go walk off that meal."

Leanne stood and started to gather the plates, but Devon put a hand on her arm and said, "That can wait, Queen Bee. Sit down a minute. I want to talk to you."

Feeling a little bit antsy being alone with Devon, Leanne walked to the opposite side of the table, and sat back down.

Devon leaned forward and said, "I've been doing some thinking about the guru's visit today. They seem to just appear from thin air and then disappear just as easily."

Leanne nodded and said, "I agree. I was thinking the same thing."

Devon continued, "Well, it got me wondering how big this island is, and if they may be staying somewhere on it. Would you be up for doing a little investigating of sorts?"

Leanne, liking where this was going, leaned forward, and said, "What did you have in mind, Romeo?"

Devon smiled wickedly and said, "Would you be up for a hike? I think they have a hidey hole somewhere on this island, and I intend to find it. I was thinking we get up at sunrise, before the others wake. And if my instincts prove right, we head northeast, and see where it takes us."

Leanne leaned back and said, "What makes you think they are northeast of here?"

Devon sat back and said, "Well, we flew in from the southwest. Since I didn't see anything, but trees and water, nor did Boy Wonder sitting up front with Chet, or he would have said something by now, don't you gather? So that only leaves the northeast end of the island we weren't able to see."

Leanne stared at him, and smiled slowly, "Very good, Romeo. Maybe there is more to you than a pretty face and a wandering willy."

Devon locked eyes with her and said, "Don't you think it's time for us to stop with the nicknames, Leanne?"

Starting to feel her insides flip, she stood, and gathered the plates. Devon stood and touched her hand. She stopped what she was doing, and responded seriously, "No, I don't. Because if we do, it is going to take us to a place I just can't go."

Devon moved a tad bit closer to her and said, "What place is that, Leanne?"

She did her best to put some distance between them and replied, "A very dangerous place. I am not one of your conquests, Devon. I am a married mother of two children. And don't look at me like that. I know what you're thinking. Until I find out where I belong, I cannot be distracted by a heartthrob musician."

Devon smiled like a school boy and said, "Okay then. We will wait and see where you belong, shall we?"

They both began clearing the table in silence. However, walking toward the house, Devon looked over at Leanne and said, "So, you think I'm a pretty face, heartthrob with a wandering willy, do you, Queen Bee?"

Leanne rolled her eyes and they both laughed.

Chapter 25

Leanne woke Monday morning at six a.m. Unable to sleep another minute longer, she got out of bed, grabbed a pair of sweats, and headed for the bathroom. She brushed her teeth and fixed her hair the best she could. For reasons unbeknownst to her, she added eyeliner and a dab of lipstick.

Looking in the mirror, she said to herself, *What the hell. Why are you putting makeup on?*

Quickly she wiped off the lipstick, but left the eyeliner. She headed back into the bedroom, changed into shorts, and a tank top. She dug through her bag for a sweatshirt, grabbed her ratty old sneakers, her backpack, and headed for the kitchen.

Once in her comfort zone, she brewed a pot of coffee while rummaging through the pantry for some food to take with them. She came up with four protein bars, a box of cereal, wheat crackers, and, for good measure, and a bag of chips. She set everything on the kitchen table and started loading her backpack, just as Devon walked into the kitchen bare chested.

Leanne looked at him and said, "I hope you plan on wearing a shirt and putting on some shoes."

Looking at his naked toes made her stomach do a little flip. She mentally smacked herself saying, *"What the hell is wrong with you."*

Devon surveyed Leanne and her surroundings and said, "Well, you've been quite the busy little beaver."

He headed for the coffee pot.

Leanne stopped him before he could pour a cup and said, "No time for that, Romeo. I'll put it in a thermos to take with us."

Devon raised an eyebrow at her and said, "Trust me, you don't want to go trapesing through the woods with me without a cup of coffee in my system. It will be worse than any bear you run up against."

Leanne huffed and said, "Fine. But take it with you while you go get dressed, and hurry it up."

Devon poured the coffee into a mug, walked up to Leanne and said, "I see someone is eager to jaunt off on our little adventure. I'll be back in a minute."

With that said, he tapped her nose with his finger, and headed out of the kitchen.

Leanne touched her nose to see if it was on fire.

Devon returned to the kitchen five minutes later; dressed in jeans, a white t-shirt, work boots, and carrying a sweatshirt.

Leanne put the bottles of water she retrieved from the fridge in the backpack and said, "Okay, let's go. I left a note for the others saying we went for a hike."

Devon looked at her, smiled slowly and said, "Well, aren't you quite the mother hen."

Leanne flipped him the bird and headed out the back door. They walked across the yard to the edge of the woods where the gurus appeared yesterday.

Devon strapped on his watch and said, "This is where they arrived from. So, I say, we head down the path a bit and see if there is another path heading northeast. My watch has a compass on it, which should help."

They walked for 15 minutes and ended up on the beach. Frustrated, Leanne said, "Shit! They could have had a boat waiting for them to get off the island."

Devon walked a few feet to his right and said, "I don't think so. Come, look."

Leanne walked over to where he was standing and said, "Those look like tire tracks."

Devon nodded, and responded, "Yes, small tire tracks. Most likely from a dune buggy or golf cart."

Excited to have found a clue, Leanne started off in the direction of the tracks and said, "Come on, let's follow them."

They walked for 20 minutes before the tracks veered off the beach and into the woods. There was a worn path that would allow a small vehicle to travel on. Devon looked at Leanne and said, "This is easier then following bread crumbs. Shall we?"

Leanne grinned wickedly and said, "Let's go find their lying asses."

They marched up the path.

Fortunately for Devon and Leanne, the path was easy to follow. Unfortunately, it was a really, really long path. It took them close to an hour to get to the end, but well worth the hike when they saw what stood before them outside of the woods.

Devon stood staring in amazement, and finally said, "Whoa. This, I did not expect."

Leanne, seething mad, replied, "Those motherfuckers! When I get my hands on them, I am personally going to choke them to death."

Devon grabbed her arm, and backed her up a few feet, "Listen, Locomotive. We have to keep our heads about us. What we need to do is calmly think this through."

Leanne, who was ready to start the Locomotives engine and steam roll right into the massive beach front compound; a sprawling two story house, with wrap around porches, gazebo, swimming pool. All the things the brochure boasted about. She took ten deep breaths, paced back and forth, and finally kicked a tree. Devon watched in amusement.

After her blood stopped boiling, she turned to Devon and said, "You're right. Let's go sit on that rock over there for a minute, so I can pull myself together."

They sat in silence on the rock for a bit. Leanne grabbed her backpack, and asked Devon, "Do you want a bottle of water?"

He looked at her to make sure she wasn't going to erupt again and said, "Sure."

Leanne reached into her backpack and brought out two bottles of water. They both drank deeply, and then Leanne said, "Okay, I'm feeling better. Let's hear what's on your mind."

Devon took another swig of water, and began, "Well, we now know they live on the island in the lap of luxury. Nonetheless, they falsely represented the living conditions to us. So I say, we take this information back to the others and devise a plan to take them down. I mean all the way down."

Leanne, nodding vigorously, said, "Yes, we expose them to the world as the fake, renowned life coaches they claim to be.

We make it so they will never work again, and do this to anyone else."

Devon, seeing the Locomotive started to rev up her engine again, grabbed Leanne's hands, stood her up, and said, "Come on, Locomotive. Let's head back."

Leanne picked up the water bottles and put them back in her back pack. Just as she was about to zip it up, her eyes shot to Devon, and she said, "Oh my God."

Concerned, Devon said, "What is it?"

Leanne put the backpack on the rock and began rummaging through it furiously. Once she found what she was looking for, she exclaimed, "Yes!"

She pulled out her cellphone.

Devon, eyeing her cautiously, said, "That's not going to do us much good out here. You heard what Blair said about no reception."

Leanne grinned wickedly and replied, "You don't need reception to take a picture. Hopefully, the battery's not dead."

She turned the phone on and saw that it had one bar of battery left. She walked to the edge of the woods and clicked, then clicked again.

Devon, standing close behind her, said, "Get a shot of the yacht moored out there in the water."

Leanne got three more shots, shut the phone off, and said, "Okay. Let's go, Romeo. When Rosalie sees these pictures, we're going to have to tie her to the clothes line."

Chapter 26

Rosalie, Amber, and Leonard were sitting at the picnic table drinking coffee, when Amber said, "What in the world have those two been up to?"

A laughing Leanne and Devon emerged from the woods.

Rosalie adjusted her body to face Leanne and Devon, and muttered, "I hope it's not what it looks like."

When Devon and Leanne reached the trio, they were out of breath and bursting with excitement.

Rosalie said, "Well, lookie here. It's the happy hikers."

Leanne, barely able to contain her herself, said, "You **are not** going to believe what we are going to tell you."

Devon sat down next to Leonard and Leanne plopped down next to Rosalie. Amber looked at Leanne, and said, "Leanne, you look like you just found a buried treasure."

Leanne excitedly said, "Oh, it's better than that. Devon, do you want to do the honors?"

Devon smiled and said, "It would be my pleasure, Queen Bee. As you all know, Leanne and I took off early this morning to take a hike..."

Feeling annoyed, Rosalie scoffed, "Oh, is that what they call it these days?"

Leanne elbowed her gently and said, "Hush. You're going to want to hear this."

Rosalie huffed and turned to Devon and said, "Okay, Horn Dog. Let's hear it."

Devon began, "Anyway, last night Leanne and I got to talking about how the gurus seem to magically appear out of the thin air and disappear just as easily. We got to thinking that they may have a hidey hole here on the island, so we decided to do some investigating. We set out this morning in search of it.

We figured since we flew in from the southwest, and none of us noticed any houses…"

Amber piped in, "Well, I know I sure didn't see anything. I had my eyes shut tight as a lid on a jar of bees, and there was no way I was opening them until we were safe and sound on the ground."

Devon, getting a little annoyed, said, "That's fine and dandy, Blondie. But my point is, with Leonard being up front with Chet, and me staring out the window of the plane in the rear, none of us saw a house. So with that known, we decided our best bet would be to head northeast. We set off down the path that the gurus emerged from and hastily departed to. We thought we might find another path leading toward the north, but we only ended up back on the beach where we were dropped off. Leanne thought that they may have had a boat waiting for them."

Leonard looked at Leanne and said, "That makes sense."

Leanne eagerly responded, "Yes, until Devon spotted a set of tire tracks in the sand!"

Rosalie arched one of her finely plucked eyebrows and said, "Really?"

Devon responded, "Yup. So we followed the tracks for approximately 20 minutes up the beach heading north. Then, at one point, they veered off into the woods. There was a very well used path leading us east…"

Leanne, bouncing in her seat, blurted out, "And we followed it!"

Devon, getting really annoyed with the interruptions, said, "Bloody hell, it's going to take me 30 days to tell this story if you keep interrupting."

Leanne looked at Devon apologetically and said, "Sorry, go on."

Devon continued, "So, as Queen Bee said, we followed it. It took us damn near an hour to get to the end of it. And when we did, we found the 'pot of gold at the end of the rainbow' as they say."

Amber looked at Devon and said, "Wait, so you actually did find a buried treasure?"

Devon put his face in his hands, and mumbled, "Bloody hell."

Leanne, just bursting at the seams, yelled, "No! We found their hidey hole!"

Rosalie, being the quick thinker that she is, turned to Leanne and said, very slowly, "You mean to tell me, that for the past six weeks, they have been living here on this island?"

Leanne, bracing herself, said, "Yes, Rosalie, that is what…"

Rosalie imploded, "Are you fucking kidding me!"

Rosalie was now standing, so Leanne stood up and said, "Rosalie, calm down…"

"Calm down! You want me to calm down after what you told us," screamed Rosalie.

Leanne, knowing exactly how Rosalie was feeling, said, "Um, yes. **But** before you explode again, you have to hear the rest of it, and then you can go kick a tree."

Amber looked at Devon and said, "Huh? Why would she want to kick a tree?"

Devon smirked and said, "Because that is what Queen Bee did."

Leonard looked at Leanne, and said, "Was the hidey hole, a shack like ours?"

Leanne scoffed and said, "Oh, no. Let me show you."

She reached into her backpack, pulled out her phone, turned it on, located the pictures, and handed the phone to Leonard.

Both Leonard and Amber gaped at the pictures and said in unison, "Holy shit!"

Rosalie ran around the table and said, "Oh, this can't be good if it has these two saying a curse word."

She reached over Leonard's shoulder, snatched the phone out of his hand, and scrolled through the pictures. Slowly, she handed the phone back to Leonard and circled the table twice, and then screamed at the top of her lungs, "I am going to fucking kill them with my bare hands. I am going to choke the life out of them!"

Devon smiled widely and said to Rosalie, "You're going to have to get in line, Pill Popper. Queen Bee, here, expressed the exact same sentiments."

Then he looked at Leanne and said, "We may have to tie her to the clothes line, after all."

Leanne quickly said to Rosalie, "Listen, Rosalie, I wanted to march straight down to that house and kick their asses, but Devon talked me out of it for good reasons."

Rosalie, not able to comprehend what Leanne was saying, replied, "I can't think of one good reason **not** to murder them in their sleep!"

Leanne understood Rosalie's anger, but calmly said, "Rosalie, sit down. Hear Devon out. The reason we didn't take action was because we wanted to come back here and tell you guys. Then, we all could devise a plan to bring them down."

Rosalie countered, "Oh, I have a plan. I say we march right back there and burn their house down!"

Rosalie paced around the table two more times, while the others watched in silence. Finally, she took a deep breath and sat down, "Okay, Horn Dog, let's hear your plan. And it better include inflicting massive amounts of pain on those two shitheads."

Devon leaned forward and said, "Oh, don't you worry, Pill Popper. We are going to hit them where it hurts. Okay, so no interrupting until you've heard me out. Then we can all add our thoughts and come up with a plan to take them down."

The others nodded, so Devon continued on, "My thought is this; we wait this out until the weekend…"

Rosalie shot up and said, "Are you kidding me? It's only Monday. How are we going to wait until the weekend? I'll have a nervous breakdown by then."

Having had enough of her, Leanne grabbed Rosalie's arm and pulled her back down onto the bench, and said, "Enough. Hear him out."

Rosalie huffed, folded her arms, and said to Devon, "Sorry. Continue."

Devon went on, "So as I was saying; we wait until the weekend. They have no intentions of returning here and they have no idea that we found their hidey hole. If we let it sit for the next five days until Saturday afternoon, we will, as the saying goes 'catch them with their panties down,' so to speak."

The group was silent for a minute until Leonard spoke up, "Devon, do you think it would be best to go there when they aren't on the island? That way, we can take a look around. If we just approach them, then we won't get a look at the inside, and I, for one, would really like to get in that house, and see how they have been living."

Rosalie and Leanne both nodded vigorously, with Leanne adding, "I agree with Leonard. I think we need all the ammunition we can get if we are going to take them all the way down."

Taking her chances, Rosalie piped in, "I also want a look at the inside of that house. It has to be worth at least a million dollars."

Amber, having listened to the others, said quietly, "But ya'll, won't that be breaking and entering or trespassing? We could get into big trouble."

Rosalie scoffed and said, "Ha! Who are they going to tell? They have been running this scam for years out on this island, and nobody has uncovered it yet; that is, until they brought the five of us out here. They couldn't handle us, so they abandoned us."

Leanne added, "Rosalie's right. We need to open this can of worms and see what slithers out."

Devon piped in, "Okay, let's get back to the basics, shall we? Here is what we know. They were hired by us or someone representing us, most likely based on our wealth. They dropped us on this island with the intentions of 'enlightening' us, once a week at Sunday dinner. The first meeting didn't go the way they planned, so they walked away from us. They disappeared for nearly five weeks; then show up here all sun kissed, claiming to have been on an emergency work related mission in Hawaii for two weeks. So we asked, where were you the other two and a half weeks, and were told, essentially, that it was none of our business. They have a sprawling beach side house on the other side of the island, which they use to lure potential clients via the brochure we each received. And then, house them in a shack buried deep in the woods. They have clients flown to the island by an unsuspecting Chet. However, they have a yacht they use for their own transportation. So with that laid out, I, too, would like a look inside of their hidey hole, and the only way to do that is with Plan B."

Rosalie snickered and said, "And what would Plan B entail, Romeo? Knock and ask if we could please see inside their goddamn mansion?"

Devon shot her a look and said, "No, Pill Popper. There will not be any knocking on doors. What I was going to suggest is, we all head over there tomorrow around noon. If the yacht is gone, then so will they be. If that's the case, we go in. If not, then back to Plan A; as a group, we go there on Saturday and confront them, agreed?"

"We all brought our phones, right?" asked Leonard

The group nodded.

"Good, then let's get them charged. If there is a wing and a prayer that we get reception on the other side of the island, we can call for help. But, most importantly, we can take pictures of everything we find to help bring them down."

They hashed out the remainder of the plan, and then headed inside to start the day.

Chapter 27

The following morning Leanne woke early and headed for the kitchen to make a hearty breakfast for the clan before they made the trek to the guru's hidey hole. She entered the kitchen, and found Rosalie sitting at the table with a cup of coffee; still seething mad. Leanne tip toed around her, grabbed a mug out of the cabinet, walked to the coffee pot, and poured a cup. She sat down at the table, glanced at Rosalie, who was staring out the window, and cautiously asked, "Rosalie, are you okay?"

Rosalie, slowly turned her head, and looked at Leanne. She lifted her cup of coffee, took a sip and replied, "I'm not sure. I'm still really pissed at those two shitheads for what they have done to us. But then, I'm more pissed at myself for letting it happen. The pills, I mean. I've overcome some really bad things in my life, and I know when I asked Harold for that first not so legal refill of Oxycodone, that it was wrong, but I…"

Rosalie stopped to wipe away her tears, "Just didn't care. The pills took me to a place where I didn't feel the pain in my leg or…"

She couldn't stop the tears, so she just rested her head in her hands

Leanne finished her sentence for her, "In your heart."

Rosalie grabbed a napkin, blew her nose, and nodded.

Amber, who was standing at the kitchen door, walked over and wrapped Rosalie in a hug from behind, and said, "Oh Rosalie, I know how you feel. I think we all took a wrong step and fell down the rabbit hole and couldn't find our way out."

Leanne, wiping away her own tears, said, "That is the perfect analogy, Amber. We all fell down the rabbit hole. But instead of landing in a magical place with a Mad Hatter and a talking rabbit, we ended up here on this island, with each other. It's been a long time since I have been to Church, nonetheless, asked God for a favor or two, but I honestly believe this was Devine Intervention."

Rosalie nodded.

Amber said, "Well, ya'll, if I have to thank those no good gurus for anything, it would be for bringing you two into my life, along with Devon and Leonard."

As if saying their names magically made them appear, in walked Devon and Leonard.

Leonard looked at the hens and said, "Um, are you guys okay?"

Amber let go of Rosalie and walked over to Leonard, and kissed him on the lips, "Yes, we're fine."

Devon, not fully awake yet, grabbed three mugs from the cabinet, shuffled over to the coffee pot, and poured two cups of coffee; handing one to Leonard and Amber. He then poured himself a cup. Leaning against the counter, he eyed the three hens, and said, "So what's going on, you look like Rover escaped the yard?"

The three hens looked at Devon and said, "Huh?"

Devon walked over and sat down at the table, and said, "You all look like you lost your dog, why so glum?

Amber, having perked back up, said, "Oh no, nothing like that. We were just talking about falling down the rabbit hole."

Now it was Devon and Leonard's turn to say, "Huh?"

Amber giggled and said, "Didn't ya'll ever read the book, Alice in Wonderland?"

Devon looked at Leonard, and then back at the hens, and at the same time, they said, "No."

Leanne explained, "We were just talking about how we ended up here. Alice in Wonderland is a children's story about a girl who chases a rabbit and falls into his hole, which then turns into a magical place, but in our case, it led us to this island, and each other."

Devon eyed them suspiciously and said, "Apparently, you three have found the cooking sherry."

Rosalie responded, "No, we haven't been hitting the cooking sherry. But we have been sharing our stories, and come to think of it, you are the only one that hasn't."

Devon raised an eyebrow and replied, "Certainly I have. I told you that I fancy women, and they fancy me, and well, it got a little out of control."

Leanne stared at him and said, "Really? That's your story? You fancy women, they fancy you, and you ended up on the road to enlightenment on a deserted island?"

Devon locked eyes with her. After a 30 second standoff, Rosalie broke the silence and said, "Romeo, let me ask you a question. What will happen when we leave this island? Will you go back to your old hound dog ways? Because I, for one, know that I am done with my pill popping days."

Devon met Leanne's inquisitive stare and said, "Hmm...that depends."

Rosalie countered, "Depends on what?"

Devon didn't want to say that it depended on what happens with Leanne, so he skirted around the subject by replying, "I honestly don't know. I've never been in a monogamous relationship."

Amber, wide eyed, said, "Devon, are you saying you've never had a steady girlfriend, not even in high school?"

Devon, starting to feel a little bit antsy, adjusted himself in his chair, and responded, "Nope, I dropped out of high school to join a band."

Engrossed in Devon's story, Leonard leaned forward, and asked, "The band you're with now, The British Bad Boys?"

Devon eyed the others and said, "No. I was in band back in my teens called 'The Hard On's', but we..."

Devon couldn't finish his sentence because the table erupted in hysterics. It took ten minutes for the jokes and puns to end. Annoyed, Devon got up to get more coffee and turned to the cackling group and said, staring directly at Leanne, "And one wonders why I never share."

He walked out the back door.

The other four looked at each other and felt horrible. Rosalie turned to Leanne and said, "You better go talk to him."

Leanne, not so sure that would be a good idea, said, "Why me? You started it Rosalie."

Rosalie retorted, "Because you're the one he fancies, so go out there, and make this right."

Flustered, Leanne stood up, and walked out the back door. Devon was sitting atop the picnic table. Leanne approached him and said quietly, "Devon, I'm sorry, we all are. It was very insensitive of us to make fun at your expense."

Devon wouldn't look at her, so she made a bold move and climbed up on the table, and sat hip to hip with him.

Though they weren't looking at each other, Devon said, "None of you know anything about me. You all have your laughs, but know nothing about me."

Leanne, feeling his anger, said cautiously, "That's because you don't want us to know anything about you."

Devon didn't respond. He sipped his coffee and stared off toward the woods. After a few minutes of silence, Devon spoke, not looking at Leanne, "Well, it's not a pretty story, nor one I like to talk about."

Leanne touched his arm gently and said, "Devon, why do you think the rest of us are here? None of our stories are pretty. They have roots that are strangling each and every one of us, but we are slowly cutting them away. Please, for me, won't you let us help you?"

Devon slowly turned, and looked at Leanne. He reached over and wiped a tear off her cheek. He sighed and said, "Go get the others."

Leanne smiled and squeezed his arm. She hopped off the table and walked back into the house.

Rosalie, Amber, and Leonard looked toward the door when she entered. Leanne marched over to the table, grabbed Rosalie's arm, and said, "If you open your mouth and one smart ass comment flies out, I will personally shove it back down your throat. Do you hear me?"

Stunned, Rosalie said, "Yes."

Leanne turned to the other two and said, "Come outside. Devon's ready to talk. And as I said to Rosalie, one smart ass comment and I'm coming after you."

On that note, Leanne, the Locomotive, turned and headed out the back door. Rosalie, Amber, and Leonard followed close behind.

Devon didn't look at the others. He just continued staring into the woods. After a minute, he began, "As you know, I grew up in a small village in England. I was the only child of

Laura and Simon Davis. My mum was a very timid woman, and as a small lad, I stuck close to her side. She cried often, which was always a worry to me. My father was a complete and utter ass. It wasn't until I was a bit older, maybe nine or ten, when I noticed the bruises on her. She would always wear high neck blouses with long sleeves. She was so beautiful and innocent. She would smile, but I always thought she still looked sad. One night, on my 16th birthday, I went to a local pub with my mates to play for the crowd. We were the only entertainment in the village, so some of the pub owners would hire us to play on a Friday or Saturday night. My father was at the pub that night, as he was most nights, and drunk, as always. He started shouting at us, "You suck. Get off the stage, you bloody punks." The owner of the pub, Gus, was afraid of him, so he didn't stop it. Finally my mates and I shut it down and left. I didn't go home that night. I stayed at a mate's, but the next morning, I woke early and headed home because I knew my mum would be worried sick about me. When I got to our Lane, I saw all the guards around our house. I took off running towards it as fast as I could. One of the guards grabbed hold of me and held me back while they wheeled my Mum's body past me. I kept screaming, "That's my mum, that's my mum," but the guard kept his grip on me."

As if in a trance, Devon continued, "That's when I saw him; he was being led out of the house by a guard. His hands were in restraints and his clothes were all bloodied. The guard, holding me back, said, "Your old man killed your Mum. Beat her bloody, he did."

The picnic table sat silent. Only Amber's sniffling could be heard. Devon stood and walked a few feet away. He turned toward the table with glassy eyes. He looked straight at Leanne and said, "I swore that day I would never lay a hand on a woman, unless it was with kindness and respect. But I vowed I would never allow myself to fall in love, because I had my father's blood in mine."

Leanne let the tears slowly fall from her cheeks. She wanted to run to Devon and hold him; take away all of his pain, but she couldn't move.

Rosalie quietly got up from the table, walked over to Devon, and wrapped her arms around him. Not saying a word, she just hung onto him.

Devon regained his composure, held onto Rosalie's hand, and said, "I'm not capable of being in a commitment. Not because of who I am, but because of what my father was. So, I find companionship from a distance."

Amber, having found her voice, said, "Devon, you are nothing like your father. I have a confession to make; I've had a crush on you since I first went to your concert at the Atrium in Tulsa, Oklahoma back in 2010. I have all your C.Ds. When I saw you at that airport back there in California, I wasn't sure what I was more nervous about; getting on Sadie or being on the same plane as you. When Mr. Chet sat me down in the seat next to you, well, I just thought I was going to die; one way or another. You showed me compassion when I needed it and I knew right then that you are a true gentleman.

Devon smiled slightly and said, "Amber, you are a gem. Leonard is a lucky man to have you."

He walked up to her and kissed her cheek. But being Amber, she threw her arms around his neck and hung on tight.

Leonard got up and walked over to them. He put a hand on Devon's shoulder.

Rosalie, wanting off this emotional roller coaster, cleared her throat and said, "So, are we going after those shitheads or what?"

Leanne swiped at her tears and said, "Yes, we are. But let's have breakfast first and head out around noon."

Amber, Leonard, and Rosalie headed inside. Devon walked over to Leanne, brushed away a stray tear with his thumb, and said, "Thank you, Queen Bee."

He kissed her cheek and walked toward the house.

Leanne raised her hand to her cheek and whispered, "Shit."

She headed for the house.

Chapter 28

After breakfast, the clan went off to get dressed. Leanne returned to the kitchen to fill the backpack with waters, ice tea, and left the snacks from the day before in it. Amber and Leonard were already at the kitchen table, checking all the cell phones to make sure they were charged.

Devon walked in and sat at the table. He put on his boots on, and asked Leonard, "Are the phones all powered up?"

Leonard replied eagerly, "Yup, ready to roll."

Just then, Rosalie entered the kitchen and the clan went silent. Amber looked at her and said, "What in the world?"

Rosalie, dressed like Crocodile Dundee, said, "What?"

Devon taking in the sight before him, said, "You look like Crocodile Dundee."

Trying to keep a straight face, Leanne went back to the task at hand of loading the backpack.

Amber, still stunned, said, "You brought that outfit with you?"

Rosalie, slightly miffed, responded, "Yes. Since no one told us where we were heading, I packed accordingly."

Devon, unable to hold it together, said, "And you thought, perhaps, we were going to the Outback?"

That was it. Leanne lost it. She buried her face in her hands, and shook with laughter.

Rosalie shot Devon her best stink eye, and retorted, "Bite me, Horn Dog."

And the room erupted with laughter.

Amber, composing herself, said, "Well, I love it. You look very, um, safari chic."

Amber's words brought the house down again.

Rosalie ignored them and said, "Well, if you have all had your laughs, can we please get a move on."

Leanne zipped up the backpack and said, "Yes. Let's get going. Everyone grab your cell phone."

The group did just that and headed out the back door. They walked the path to the beach and as they stepped out of the woods and onto the sand, they stopped dead in their tracks. Slowly gliding to the dock was Chet and Sadie. Once Chet shut down the engine, he hopped out of the plane onto the dock, followed closely by two mutts.

Amber squealed with delight and ran toward the dock. She was greeted by Bella and Blaze with wagging tails and friendly barks. She bent down, and rubbed their heads, cooing, "Aren't you so cute. Yes, you are."

Chet caught up to them and said, "Bella, Blaze, heel."

Both dogs stopped licking Amber and sat down, tails wagging.

Amber gave Chet a wide smile and said, "What a great surprise!"

She hugged him.

The other four caught up to them on the dock. Leonard shook Chet's hand and said hello. Then joined Amber by petting the dogs.

Rosalie greeted Chet, "Am I glad to see you."

Leanne looked at Chet, then at the hounds and said, "I'm so glad you decided to visit, like we talked about."

The others looked from Leanne to Chet with questioning eyes.

Chet said, "Well, I got to thinking about what ya'll said about the Claine's when I dropped off the last food supply. And when I didn't hear from those two, I thought I should come back out here and check on ya'll."

Devon reached over and patted Chet's shoulder, and said, "That's quite nice of you to fly all the way out here to check up on us. However, at the moment, we have a little situation that has occurred."

Rosalie scoffed and said, "Ha! A little situation? I would call it more like the war of the century, when I get my hands on those two!"

Devon ignored Rosalie, and continued, "You see, Chet. Leanne and I got to wondering. Since you weren't flying the

Claine's to and from the island, that they may have a place somewhere here on the island."

Chet took off his cap and ran his fingers through his hair, and said, "Well, that ain't ever occurred to me. But now that you mention it, it could be a possibility."

Again, Rosalie scoffed and said, "Oh, it's more than a possibility. Leanne and Devon found their hidey hole. And when I get my hands on them, they are going to wish they never met me!"

Leanne put a hand on Rosalie's arm and said, "Why don't you let Devon finish telling Chet the story and then we can be on our way."

Rosalie took a deep breath and said, "Okay, sorry. Go on."

Devon continued, "So, as Rosalie mentioned, Leanne and I did find their house and…"

Rosalie butted in again, "House? It's a goddamn million dollar sprawling estate!"

All eyes turned to her. She shuffled her feet and looked at the ground and said, "Sorry, go on."

Devon raised an eyebrow at her and then turned back to Chet, "So, you see, we were just heading that way to get a better look, you could say."

Chet rubbed his chin, and asked, "Where about is this place?"

Leanne piped in, "It's down the beach about 20 minutes, then you turn down a path into the woods; a really, really long path. It took Devon and I almost an hour to get there."

Chet, rubbing his chin again, said, "Well, I'd be happy to fly ya'll over there."

Rosalie was all for that, but Devon, replied, "No, I think it might be better if we go on foot. What we're hoping for is that they have left the island and we can get a look around."

Chet considered this and said, "Well, if ya'll don't mind me and the hounds tagging along, I'd be mighty interested in seeing it myself."

Concerned, Amber said to Chet, "Mr. Chet, it could be like five miles or more from here. Are you sure you're up for that?"

Chet bellowed out one of his rare laughs and said, "Little Lady, Bella, Blaze, and me, we go hiking ten miles every chance we get. There ain't nothin' they like better than a good hunt."

Well, that settled it. Chet was joining the group. They set off down the beach, Bella and Blaze leading the pack.

It took them over an hour to get to the edge of the woods, overlooking the guru's house. Rosalie, Amber, Leonard and Chet all stared in amazement. Chet finally broke the silence, and declared, "Well, I'll be damned."

Rosalie followed with, "Are you fucking kidding me? Leanne, your pictures didn't tell the whole story."

Amber and Leonard said nothing. They just stood there, wide eyed, with their mouths hanging open.

Devon backed the group away from the edge and back toward the woods. He turned to Leanne and said, "Queen Bee, go take another look and see if the yacht is gone."

Leonard, finally able to speak, said, "I'll go with her and see if I can spot any security cameras."

Devon slapped him on the back and said, "Brilliant idea, Boy Wonder."

Leanne and Leonard crept low to the edge of the woods and down the slope, about 50 feet to get a better look.

Leanne looked around and whispered to Leonard, "The yacht's gone. Want to take a closer look for security cameras?"

Leonard smiled at her, rubbed his hands together, and said, "Oh boy, do I."

They made a mad dash down the hill, across the expansive green grass to the side of the house. Leanne bent over, rested her hands on her knees, trying to catch her breath. She looked over at Leonard, who didn't even break a sweat and said, "I haven't had this much fun since high school."

Leonard laughed and said, "I've never had this much fun."

He reached into his back pocket and pulled out what looked like a wallet; however, when he opened it, Leanne saw a tiny set of tools.

She asked him, "What's that?"

Leonard grinned wickedly, and responded, "Oh, just a few handy tools, in case I ever have to disarm a security system and break into a house. Must be the computer geek in me. I've had them since I was a boy. I was always taking apart any electronic I could get my hands on."

Leanne high fived him and they snuck around to the back of the house. Leonard located the security box and went to work. Five minutes later, he said, "All clear. I put a block on the timer so there won't be a time lapse in the video. And I erased the last half hour, just in case."

Leanne high fived him again and said, "Let's go get the others."

They walked back to the side of the house and waved the others down. Blaze and Bella came barreling down the slope and ran right to them. It took the others a bit longer because of the complaining Crocodile Dundee.

Once she caught up to Leanne and Leonard she said, out of breath, "Jesus H. Christmas, you gave us all a heart attack sneaking around down here."

Leanne smiled and said, "I didn't see the yacht. So, Boy Wonder and I decided to get the alarm and security cameras turned off before you guys came into view."

Devon patted Leonard on the back and said, "Good going, mate. Do you think you can get us into the house?"

Leonard flashed a wicked grin and held up his handy dandy tool set, and said, "No problem."

The eight of them, being the addition of Chet and the two hounds, walked around to the back of the house.

Rosalie said, "Geez, this is like that show Let's Make a Deal. Should we pick door number one, two, or three?"

The others looked at her and said, "Huh?"

Only Chet knew what she was talking about and said, "Me and my Annie used to watch that program. I was always picking the wrong door."

Devon laughed and said, "Then we'll leave it to Boy Genius here to pick, shall we?"

Leonard looked at all three doors and chose the one in the middle, which was a set of French doors off the patio. He walked up to the door, selected a few tools from the case, and went to work. Three seconds later, he had the doors open, and no alarms blaring. The rest of the group, five feet behind him, let out a collective sigh of relief.

Devon said to the group, "Okay, let's do it like this; split up. Take pictures of everything, and for the love of the Queen, don't touch anything."

Rosalie snickered and said, "And 'for the love of what Queen' might that be Brit?"

Devon smirked and replied, "Bite me, Pill Popper."

Leanne, wanting this bantering to stop, said, "Enough, let's go. Chet, will the dogs be okay out here?"

Chet turned to the hounds and said, "Stay," and answered, "Yup."

The group headed inside to what looked like a hotel ballroom. Devon told Leonard and Amber to head upstairs, Devon and Rosalie took the left wing and Leanne and Chet took the other side of the house. After 25 minutes, the group reconvened in the room they entered through. Everyone started talking at once.

Devon told them, "Save it for the walk back. It's time to get the bloody hell out of here."

They exited the house single file. Leonard, the last one out, relocked the doors from the outside and then ran over to the security box, and told the others, "Head back up back to the woods. Once you're out of sight, I'll start the cameras and turn on the alarm."

Amber, looking concerned, said, "But then you'll be the only one they see on it."

Leonard smiled at Amber and said, "I'm going to set it on a ten minute delay, which is plenty of time for me to make it back to the woods,"

He kissed her smack on the lips and said, "Go."

True to his word, Leonard was up the hill, and safely in the woods in seven minutes flat. Once he reached the others, he flopped down on the ground and said breathless, "Going down the hill was a lot easier than coming up."

Leanne handed him a bottle of water and said, "You did good, Leonard. Thank you."

The group sat in silence and drank the remainder of their water. When they were finished, Leanne collected the bottles, put them in the backpack, and said, "Let's head back to the cabin, and I'll fix us a huge lunch."

Looking at Chet, she said, "And I'm not taking no for answer from you. You're one of us now; thick as thieves."

That got a laugh from the group.

Chet replied, "I'd like that Leanne, that's right kind of you."

He gave her a wink.

Two hours later, the clan was gathered around the picnic table eating hamburgers, hot dogs, and pasta salad. Leanne cooked a couple extra burgers and dogs for the hounds. Showing their appreciation, they stayed right by her side.

Devon finished his hamburger and said to Chet, "May I ask you something, Chet?'

Chet finished chewing and replied, "Well, considering we're thick as thieves, can't say that I'd mind."

That brought a chuckle from the others.

Devon asked, "Did you do the food shopping for the last delivery?"

Eyeing the group, Chet cleared his throat and said, "Well, um, you see, those Claine's gave me one list, and told me I was to buy the same things every month. But when I got a look at Country Girl here, all skin and bones, and Miss Firecracker, over there," pointing his chin at Rosalie, "And Mama Bear," looking at Leanne, "I said to myself, Chet, these folks ain't like the others that come here. This group will be needing something other than rabbit food. So with my Annie guiding me from up above, I bought what I thought would be good for the soul, so to speak."

Leanne placed her hand on top of Chet's and said with affection, "I think I can speak for all of us, when I say, thank you. Thank you for caring enough about us to make that decision and go against what the gurus told you to do."

Rosalie agreed, and added, "Chet, you said we're not like the others. What did you mean by that?"

Chet pushed his plate away and said to Leanne, "Leanne, that was a mighty good meal. Don't remember the last time I had a home cooked meal. So, thank you."

He turned to Rosalie and replied, "Well, Miss Rosalie, the others I've brought here are hard to describe. They were all real tan, real skinny, and mean as rattlesnakes. I would usually go fetch the same four, every three months or so. Fly them up from SoCal Airport, but never brought them back. Those Claine's, they would meet us at the dock, same as you; but with these other folks, it was all hugs and kisses when they arrived."

Deep in thought, Chet rubbed his chin and said, "Come to think of it, the Claines always had a golf cart with them when they picked up those folks. And I never delivered food to them neither."

Chet looked around the table, and continued, "I never paid no mind. Picked them up, dropped them off on this here island; but I'll tell you one thing, I never took a liking to them. But there was something different about you five that stuck in my craw. I just knew you were different, so that's why I flew back out here today, and I'm dang glad I did, after seeing what we seen."

Amber smiled and said, "Well, we're all glad you did, too. I just worry about you flying all this way by yourself."

Chet smiled back at Amber and said, "Don't you worry, Little Lady. I've been flying longer then you've been born; plus, my place is just on the other side of this island; a short 20 minute flight."

Rosalie's ears perked up, and she asked Chet, "Are you saying the mainland is only 20 minutes away? How come you never saw that monstrosity of a house back there on the beach?"

Chet sat back and said, "Well, I reckon it's because the mainland is southeast of here. And whenever I fly the Claine's people in, I come up from Cali. Never been no need to fly to the north end of the island."

Chet, leaned forward and looking confused, said, "But come to think of it now, when my Annie was alive, some years ago, we would take Sadie for a joy ride. That's what my Annie would call it. She would say to me every Sunday after church, "Chet, let's take a joy ride and look at all of God's wonders," so, every Sunday, we would hop in Sadie and fly over the islands and the waters surrounding them. We had to have flown over this here island a hundred times, and I ain't never seen that, monstrosity, as you call it. Like I said though, it's been ten years since my Annie passed on, and I never did another joy ride since."

Seeing the sadness in Chet's eyes, Amber quietly said, "You miss her something awful, don't you? Do you have any children?"

Chet took off his cap and placed it in his lap. He ran his fingers through his snow white hair, replaced his cap, cleared his throat, and said, "Yup, miss her every day that goes by, that's the only reason I keep flying. It brings me just that much closer to her. As for kids, nope, not in the cards for Annie and I. But I do have my fur babies here: Bella and Blaze."

Hearing their names, the hounds walked over, and sat on either side of Chet.

Amber wiped away a tear, walked over to Chet, hugged him from behind, and said, "Well, you got us now. We're your family, too."

The other four agreed.

Chet patted Amber's hand and said, "Thank you, Country Girl, that's mighty kind of you to say. My Annie, she would have taken a shining to all of you."

Devon sat back, quietly taking in all of what Chet had to say, filing it away for another time.

Chet stood and said, "Well, I think it's time me and the kids here, head back home. Leanne, thank you kindly for this meal."

Looking at the group, he added, "So, what do ya'll reckon you're going to do about those Claine folks?"

Rosalie, not missing a beat, said, "Kill them."

The others shot her a look, and she said, "What?"

Devon replied to Chet's question, "Well, we haven't worked out all the details yet. Our plan is to go back on Saturday and confront them."

Leanne piped in, "That's if they are even there. I, for one, don't want to keep hiking back and forth to find out."

Chet rubbed his chin and said, "Well, how about this? I can do a fly over Saturday morning, and if I see that big boat of theirs, I can come back by and let ya'll know."

Leanne smiled and said, "That would be terrific. If they are there, you and the dogs can come with us to confront them, considering they used you to fly us out here. We can go in as a united front."

Everyone agreed, and the plan was set to meet Chet back on the beach Saturday morning at ten a.m.

Chapter 29

The next three days crawled by at a snail's pace. The group used the time to straighten up the cabin and get their things in order in anticipation of their pending departure off the island. Rosalie, the chattiest of the group, kept saying, "I can't wait to get off this hell hole. When I get home, I am going to take the longest, hottest shower in my life, and then I am going to curl up in my big comfy bed and sleep for a week straight."

The others listened to her, but never mentioned their plans. Finally, when Saturday morning arrived, the clan gathered in the kitchen early, for what was most likely going to be their final breakfast together. Leanne was at the stove frying up bangers, while Devon whisked eggs to be scrambled. Leonard and Amber sat at the table sipping their coffee.

Rosalie, not able to stand another second of this somber group, said, "What the hell is wrong with all of you? Do you realize we are less than 12 hours away from getting off this island?"

Being met with complete silence, Rosalie prodded Amber and Leonard, "Love birds, what are your plans when you leave here?"

Amber smiled at Rosalie and said, "I'd like to go home; to the farm, I mean."

Rosalie cheerfully said, "That's great, are you taking Brainiac here with you?"

Leonard, feeling a little bit awkward, shifted in his seat and said, "Um, well, we haven't really discussed that yet."

Rosalie, wide eyed, said, "What the hell are you waiting for? Amber, do you want Leonard to come home with you and meet your family?"

Amber fiddled with a napkin, looked up at Rosalie, and said, "Yes, I do, but, I'm not sure if that's what Leonard wants."

Rosalie, being the barracuda that she is, said, "Well, for Christ sake, turn to Leonard, and tell him, not me."

Amber, nervous as a fish in a barrel, turned to Leonard, and said, "Um, Leonard, do you want to come home with me and meet Momma and Daddy, and the rest of the Quinn clan?"

Leonard smiled at her, took her hand, and replied, "Yes, I do. I want to meet your parents and siblings. But most of all, I want to spend the rest of my life with you. I would be happy to go to Oklahoma with you, so I can ask your daddy face to face, if he would give me his blessing to marry his baby daughter."

Amber, with tears streaming down her face, leaned over and kissed him, and said, "I love you and so will my daddy."

Leonard, feeling more confident, said to Amber, "Okay, then, why don't we fly from Seattle back to L.A? Get our things packed up, and I'll drive us to Oklahoma."

Rosalie, pleased with herself, said, "Don't forget about a ring. You are going to need that to prove your intentions to Country Girl's daddy."

Leonard, starting to look a tad pale, said, "Um, we can buy one in L.A before we leave. Does that sound okay, Amber?"

Amber grabbed hold of his hand and said, "It sounds perfect."

Devon, having been quiet during all of that, said, "Well, I do believe you two kids just got engaged. Congratulations!"

Leanne, with concern in her eyes, walked over to the happy couple, and asked, "Amber, where are you going to tell your parents you met Leonard?

Amber looked at Leanne and replied, "I'm going to tell them the truth. You don't lie to Momma or else you'll end up cleaning the chicken coop for a month."

Pleased to hear that, Leanne hugged her and said, "Congratulations, I am so happy for the both of you."

Fluffing up her hen feathers, Rosalie turned to Devon, and asked, "So what about you, Rock Star? What are your plans? Off to tour the world with the band?"

Devon occupied himself pouring the eggs into the skillet. With his back to the others, he answered Rosalie, "Not sure what my plans are yet. Our tour dates don't begin until late October; I have plenty of time to hash things out."

Rosalie, deciding not to push any further with Devon, turned to Leanne and said, "What about you, Locomotive? You must be excited to get off this island and home to your family."

Leanne, back at the stove, plated the bangers, set them on the counter, and took five plates out of the cabinet. Considering her response, she carefully replied, "Yes, I'm very excited to get home to Luke and Lindsey. Not a day has gone by that I haven't missed them with all my heart."

Rosalie, being Rosalie, asked, "What about your husband?"

Leanne set out the plates, and with a slight laugh said, "Well, that will be a work in progress, which I will take one day at a time."

Wanting off this subject, Devon announced, "Eggs are ready."

He set the platter on the table.

They ate in silence. When everyone was finished, Devon said to the others, "Since Rosalie here is such an eager beaver to get off the island, why don't the rest of you go get ready. Rosalie and I will clean up."

Rosalie shot him a look, but what she saw on his face, in return, made her change her tactics, and said, "Fine, I'm already dressed. You guys go ahead and I'll help Devon."

Leanne, Leonard, and Amber agreed and headed out of the kitchen. Devon and Rosalie began clearing the dishes. Keeping an eye on Devon, Rosalie walked over, and placed the dishes in the sink. After a minute of silence, she turned to Devon and said, "Okay, spill it, Romeo. I see those wheels turning in your head."

Devon turned to her and said, "Well, actually, there is something I wanted to discuss with you, but I would appreciate it if we could keep this between you and me."

Feeling the hairs on the back of her neck tingle, Rosalie said, "Okay, I can do that. What's on your mind?"

Devon wiped his hands on the dish towel and replied, "Let's sit a minute."

Rosalie took the dish towel from him, dried her hands, and sat.

Devon began, "I've come to a decision of how to bring the guru's down, and it will require your help."

Her interest being peaked, Rosalie sat back, folded her arms across her chest, and said, "I'm listening."

Devon leaned forward and said, "Well, we know they are running a scam of sorts, and coming to know what I know of them, I believe they hold their reputation as renowned life coaches to the rich and famous in the highest regard. So, with that in mind; if we were to go public on what happened to us here, I believe they would be a tad past scared shitless that their reputation would be tarnished and, more important, their wealth would all go bye-bye."

Rosalie agreed with him. Devon continued, "This is where you come in. I want to take their house from them."

Rosalie sat up, leaned forward, and asked, "How?"

Devon smiled slowly and replied, "I want to buy that monstrosity of a house of theirs."

Rosalie said, "Are you crazy!"

Devon quickly said, "Hush. I don't want the others to hear. If you listen to me, you might like the idea. When we confront them today, I am going to lay it all out for them as such, "If you don't want us to go public with who and what you really are; that being frauds, then I would like to make a deal with you," something to that effect. And because my intention is to never have them use this island again for their scamming ways as life coaches, I want to buy it."

Rosalie sat back and stared at Devon straight in the eyes, and finally said, "Hmm…I think there is more to this, Romeo, but, hey, I'll play along. I gather you want me to come up with a number to throw at them?"

Devon leaned back and replied, "Precisely. I plan on today ending with a signed agreement to sell me the house and them sailing off into the sunset. Then, after all is said and done, I will fly over to Seattle with you and the others, contact my attorney and my manager, and have the deal finalized in time to throw a magnificent wedding for Boy Genius and Country Girl here on the island."

Now, it was Rosalie's turn to slowly smile. After a few minutes of digesting everything that Devon laid out on the table, she leaned forward and said, "Rock Star, I'm going to say something, and I don't want you to take it the wrong way, but, I think I just fell a tad bit in love with you."

Devon grinned and said, "It happens."

They both laughed.

The gang was all packed up and eager to go meet Chet at the beach. Rosalie, hell bent on getting off the island today, said, "I think we should bring our bags to the beach with us, and load them onto Sadie before we hike over to the guru's hidey hole."

Leanne, concerned about how the confrontation with Blair and Micah might go, said, "Why don't we leave them here for now and we can come back for them after."

Amber, not one to argue, said, "I don't know. I think we should take them with us; get them loaded on Sadie, so we can leave straight from the beach before it gets dark."

Devon and Leonard agreed. Leonard added, "We could stay at a hotel in Seattle tonight, and fly back to L.A. in the morning."

Out voted, Leanne reluctantly agreed.

Rosalie, ready to get the show on the road, said, "Come on. Let's get a move on. Chet said he would meet us at ten and its quarter of."

Everyone grabbed their bags and headed to the door. Leanne, the Locomotive, being the caboose, hesitated to shut the back door.

Devon, waiting for her at the bottom of the stairs, said gently, "Leanne."

She pulled the back door closed and with tears in her eyes, walked down the stairs.

Chapter 30

It took the clan 15 minutes to get to the beach. And to the surprise of the others, there was no usual complaining or griping from Rosalie. Once they emerged from the woods, they spotted Chet and the hounds on the beach. Chet was throwing a piece of driftwood into the water and Blaze and Bella were racing after it.

Amber yelled out, "Hi there, Chet!"

The hounds heard her voice and ran up the beach to greet her; shaking the water off their fur. Amber laughed and kneeled down in the sand for some doggie kisses.

Leonard walked over and joined her, and said, "We're definitely getting a dog when we're married. My parents would never allow it when I was a kid."

Amber kissed him and said, "Well, our kids are going to have dogs and the best daddy in the whole world."

Stunned, silent at the mention of kids, Leonard just smiled.

Rosalie dragged her bag up to the dock, and greeted Chet, "Hello there, Chet. We thought we would bring our bags with us and load them onto Sadie so we can hit the skyways, lickety-split, after we slaughter the gurus."

Devon and Leanne approached behind Rosalie and said, "Hello," to Chet.

Devon, eager to know, asked Chet, "So, Chet my man, are they there or not?"

Chet smiled and said, "Yes, Sir. That big ole boat of theirs is sitting right out there in the Puget Sound. Can't say I saw any sign of life, but they're there."

Always on her toes, Rosalie said, "Ha! If they're not dead, they will be when I get my hands on them."

Devon shot her a look and said, "Let's keep the big picture in focus, shall we?"

Rosalie nodded and said, "Don't worry, Horn Dog. My bark is worse than my bite."

Devon scoffed and said, "That, I doubt. Shall I ask Harold?"

Rosalie flipped him the bird and walked over to Amber and Leonard.

Leanne, being uncharacteristically quiet, said, "Okay, let's load our bags onto Sadie, and go get this over with."

She followed Chet up the dock, to the plane, climbed aboard, and put her bags on one of the two front seats. Devon followed in behind her and tossed his bag onto the seat next to hers and said, "Lucky for you it's a short flight." He tapped her nose and walked off Sadie.

Touching her tingling nose, Leanne whispered, "Oh, boy."

After Amber, Leonard, and Rosalie loaded their bags aboard Sadie, the group of eight set off down the beach to confront the gurus. It took the group close to an hour and a half to get to the edge of the woods overlooking the massive house. They had to devise a game plan of how to approach Blair and Micah. Rosalie was all for storming the castle with swords drawn, but the others reeled her in with logic.

Amber stepped up and suggested, "Why don't we just walk down there, knock on the door, and see what happens."

Leanne, not sure she was up for this, said, "I don't have a good feeling about this. They were really angry the last time they were at the cabin."

Rosalie walked up to Leanne, grabbed her by the shoulders, and said, "Locomotive, you have got to pull it together. Remember the last six weeks. Remember you have been torn away from your babies for six weeks. Now it's time to pull your shit together and help us bring them down."

Leanne said, "I know, I know. But I'm scared. Not of those two idiots, but of not having all of you around me. I've come to count on you, and I just don't know if I can go back to L.A. and be this strong and confident; especially, when it comes to dealing with Blake."

Rosalie stepped back and looked at the others, and said, "Take out your cell phones."

The others did as they were told.

Then Rosalie said, "Tell me your numbers." and they did, one by one.

Rosalie programmed them into her phone, turned to Leanne, and said, "I am going to text you these numbers. That way, if you need us, all you have to do is call. I am only 15 minutes from you in L.A. I will be there in a heartbeat if you need me."

Amber walked over to Leanne, and hugged her, then said, "I might be in Oklahoma. But you can bet your britches, if you need me, I'll come running."

Knowing how Leanne was feeling, Devon hoped more than ever that his plan didn't backfire, so he said, "I agree with Amber. Let's walk up to the front door and see what happens."

The other five nodded and headed down the slope. They crossed the lawn as a united front, climbed the front porch stairs. Devon took a deep breath and knocked loudly on the front door. After a few minutes of no response, he knocked more vigorously. A minute later, the front door opened and Micah and Blair stood in front of the angry group, wide eyed and speechless.

Rosalie stepped forward and said, "Trick or treat, gurus."

The Prom King and Queen just stood there stunned.

Leanne, the Locomotive, pushed forward and said, "Surprised? Well you can't possibly be more surprised than we were when we found your hidey hole. Now step aside, we're coming in."

Blair, recovering quickly, said, "The hell you are."

Micah, having found his tongue stuttered, "But how did you find us?"

Devon smiled and responded, "Oh, it was easy enough. We followed your tire tracks down the beach after your last visit to us. Now, as Leanne said, step aside, we have some business to tend to." He pushed through the door, with the pack following close behind him.

Once inside, Blair, angrier than a swarm of bees, screamed, "You can't just barge in here. Get out of my house!"

Devon smiled and said, "Not going to happen, Red. We've got some business to discuss and you are going to shut up and listen. So, let's go find somewhere to sit, shall we?"

Blair, practically frothing at the mouth, said, "You are not going to sit down anywhere in my house, and we are definitely not having a discussion with you!"

Chet stepped forward and said, "Well, Claines, we can do this the easy way or the hard way. Either you sit down and hear these folks out, or I fly them back to the mainland and contact the authorities. Your choice."

Micah, nervous as a cat on a hot tin roof, said to Blair, "Maybe we should hear what they have to say."

She looked at Chet, and screamed, "You traitor! We pay you good money to fly our clients out here! You would have nothing if it wasn't for us, except your pitiful trailer and those nasty mutts. Don't cross us or you will be very sorry!"

Chet took off his cap, ran his fingers through his hair, replaced his cap, and said, "Well, now the way I see it, you had me doing your dirty work. Paid me some, you did, but if I had known what crooks you were, I wouldn't have taken a plug nickel from the likes of you. Now if you ain't interested in hearing these folks out, like I said before, I'd be happy to fly them outta here and bring back the authorities."

Micah, knowing full well what would happen if the police started digging into their business, let alone their past, said to Blair, "Let's sit down and hear what they have to say."

Blair shot him daggers with her eyes, but he shot back, "Now."

They all moved into the spacious living room with high ceilings, a floor to ceiling fireplace, and a set of floral couches.

Fuming mad, Blair sat down on one of the couches, with Micah following closely.

Devon, Leanne, Amber, and Leonard sat across from them on the other couch. Rosalie and Chet stood to the side, close to the door. Rosalie leaned over to Chet and whispered, "Come with me, I need to check something out."

They inched their way out the door until Blair barked, "Where do you two think you're going?" Don't you dare step foot in any other part of this house!"

Chet smiled and said, "No, ma'am, we're just going to check on my hounds."

They scurried out the front door. Once outside, Chet turned to Rosalie, and asked, "What you got up your sleeve there, Firecracker?"

Rosalie smiled and said, "I need to get a look at the property."

Chet rubbed his chin, and said, "Well, seeing as I did a fly over earlier, I can tell you that there is a whole other part of this house on the north end; plus, the big one out there by the pool."

Rosalie smiled wickedly and said, "Well then, why don't we go take a peek?"

They walked to the north side of the house with the hounds on their heels. Rosalie whistled when they stopped in front of the expansive wing attached to the main house. With her realtor radar on high alert, she said, "That's got to be at least four thousand square feet," and by counting the windows added, "Six bedrooms."

They walked around the perimeter of the house until they reached the pool area. Chet took off his cap, ran his fingers through his hair, and said, "Why do you reckon those two need all this space? That, there, pool house is way bigger than the shack in the woods they holed ya'll up in."

Rosalie's mental calculator was clicking away. She turned to Chet and said, "Okay, I've got what I need. Let's head back inside."

They walked in the front door and could hear Blair yelling at the top of her lungs, "No fucking way! You are all bat shit crazy!"

Chet and Rosalie entered the room. Devon looked at Rosalie and she held up a two and a five with her fingers. Devon raised an eyebrow, cleared his throat, and said, "Okay, here's what I'm offering, I'll buy this house for two point five million…"

Before he could finish, Blair jumped up off the couch, and screeched, "Are you insane? This house is worth at least five million!

The other four being Leanne, Amber, Leonard, and Chet stared at Devon in astonishment.

Amber, under her breath, said, "Good Lord."

Rosalie smiled smugly at Blair and said, "Red, I would truly consider Devon's offer. Being that I am a five star, top tier realtor in one of the biggest cities in the country, I know fair market value, and two point five million is more than fair market value for this house."

Blair snorted at Rosalie, "You are nothing more than a miserable, lonely, pill popping spinster. Don't you tell me about fair market value!"

Devon stood and said, "Okay, well, if that's how you want to play it, we'll be off then."

The others stood to leave.

This time it was Micah who stood and said, "Wait!"

He turned to Blair and said, "We can't let them leave here. They'll destroy us…"

Blair shot back at him, "Shut the hell up, Micah."

Micah volleyed back, "No, you shut the hell up, Blair. I'm not letting you call the shots anymore. If it wasn't for your hot headed temper, we wouldn't be in this mess. If they go back to the mainland and start digging, you know what will happen to us. And I, for one, am not going to jail for you or anyone else."

Still stunned by Micah's backlash, Blair turned to Devon and said, "You think you're so smart, Lover Boy. You think you can walk in here and throw around your Rock Star money. Well, you have sadly misjudged me. I know your type. I've been surrounded by the likes of you all my life; rich, pretty boys just wanting to get into your pants. Well, you are not taking what I have worked so hard for. I climbed out of the gutter to get where I am and nobody is going to take that away from me!"

Rosalie smiled slowly, stepped closer to Blair and said, "Ah, so now we know. You're nothing more than a street rat; clawing your way up and over the bodies to get to the top. Well, let me tell you something, Red, you've met your match with me. I know where to look for the skeletons, so take a good look at our faces, because they are going to be in every one of your nightmares when you are rotting away in prison."

Blair, shaking with anger, looked around at the others and said, "You are nothing. You will all leave here and go back to your sorry, pitiful, miserable lives. You can't touch me."

This time it was Leonard who spoke up and said to Blair, "You might want to take another look at our faces, Blair. I'm the only child of one of the richest men in the country. Devon is a famous Rock Star. Rosalie owns one of the largest real estate companies in L.A. Leanne is married to a powerful attorney and Amber is adored by the rich and famous Hollywood crowd you prey on. We do have the power and will use every ounce of it to bring you down. Trust me, I'm betting the house on it."

Micah, pale as a ghost, said to Blair, "Just sell him the stupid, fucking house. We can take the yacht and sail to anywhere in the world. We don't need this, we have each other, always have, always will. Please, let's just get out of here."

Blair looked at him with tears streaming down her face. Micah put his arm around her and said to the others, "We're going to pack. I'll give you our attorney's number. I'll request that all of our belongings be moved to storage on the main land. But, believe me, when I tell you this, there will be rock solid conditions attached to any agreement."

Devon raised an eyebrow and asked, "Such as?"

Micah got in Devon's face and said with contempt, "If you so much as utter our names to the press, or anybody else for that matter, that will brings us embarrassment, disgrace, or harm, you will regret it. Believe me when I say, I will make it my life's mission to destroy each and every one of you."

With that said, Micah led Blair out of the room, and up the stairs.

Chapter 31

They decided to wait up in the woods for the gurus to depart. Devon turned to Rosalie, and asked, "Do you think you could stay on in Seattle for a couple of days to help me sort through the details of the purchase?"

Rosalie considered him for a minute and replied, "Sure, Rock Star. I've got nowhere to be at the moment."

Devon smiled and said to the others, "If you guys are okay with this, I'd like to wait until those two are merrily on their way. Then, I need to go back down there and take look around, and see exactly what the bloody hell I just bought."

That brought a dose of well needed laughter to the clan.

Rosalie said, "Well, all I know is, you got a hell of a deal, because I threw you a low ball. I'm thinking it may be worth close to five million; but given the circumstances, I felt the gurus would bite at two point five and run with it, which they did with a little nudging from Boy Wonder over there."

Leonard, sitting on the ground with Amber by his side, smiled and said, "I guess I must have learned something from my father. I've spent most of my life watching him maneuver and manipulate through business dealings, so, I guess, when the big guns are needed, that's how you do it."

Amber elbowed him gently and said, "Don't think you'll ever get away with that with me. I've got bigger guns than you, got it?"

Leonard wrapped an arm around her and pulled her close, and said, "Got it."

* * *

It took the gurus close to two hours to pack, boarded the yacht and sailed off into the horizon. The clan headed down the hill, across the vast lawn and up the stairs to the front porch. Devon turned the door knob only to find it locked. He looked at Leonard and said, "Boy Wonder, do you think you could help me out here?"

Leonard looked at the door and said, "Let me run around back to the door we opened the other day, it will be quicker."

Before he could take one step, Amber grabbed his arm, looked at the others, and said with concern, "Ya'll, you don't think they rigged a bomb to the house, do you?"

They looked at her and considered what she said.

Rosalie replied, "Hmm, good question. I never thought of that, but now that you mention it, it could be a possibility."

Chet rubbed his chin and said, "Naw. They ain't got the brains for that, or the time. It would take at least eight hours to build even a small bomb."

All eyes, wide as saucers, were on Chet. He looked at them and laughed, and said, "I was in a war or two in my time; ammunitions were my specialty until I finished flight school and then it was all about the bird."

Relieved to hear this, they relaxed. Amber released Leonard's arm and he took off down the stairs, and headed around to the back of the house.

It took him exactly three minutes to open the front door for them. Rosalie asked Leonard, "Hey, Magic Fingers, you think you can come with me to the other side of the house and get me in?"

They all looked at Rosalie. Devon raised an eyebrow, and asked, "What other side of the house?"

Rosalie laughed and replied, "Ha, with all of the excitement I forgot to mention it. There is approximately a four thousand square foot addition on the north side of this house. From the outside, I'd guess there are about six bedrooms."

Amber squealed, "Good golly. With seven bedrooms in this house, that makes 13 in total."

Rosalie smiled, and added, "Oh, I'm betting there are four more in that pool house out back."

Chet whistled and said to Devon, "Son, I'm thinking you didn't buy a house, more like a hotel."

Devon smiled slowly, looked at Rosalie, and said, "Perfect."

Rosalie, eager to get a look inside the other half of the house and the pool house, said, "Well, let's go take a look."

The clan descended the stairs and headed around to the north side of the house. Once there, Leonard worked his magic, popped the lock, and stepped aside for the group to move forward into the house. They entered the foyer and stopped dead in their tracks. Rosalie, breaking the silence, said, "Whoa, this looks like one of those boutique hotels in Miami."

Devon agreed. The clan continued through the house of white and aqua, with floor to ceiling windows, and tropical print couches. They canvassed the whole first floor, which included a huge kitchen, a solarium, theatre room, spa, and the best part, for Devon, a recording studio; completely sound proofed. They headed upstairs to the bedrooms, and Rosalie nailed it. There were six spacious bedrooms, and six bathrooms. The Master bedroom was ginormous, with a huge walk in closet. They checked out all the bedrooms and then headed back down stairs.

Amber, still stunned, said, "Geez Louise, they sure did make a lot of money life coaching."

Rosalie scoffed and said, "Ha! Is that what you call it? I call it life scamming!"

They locked up the apparent guest house and moved on to the pool house in the back. Leonard picked the lock as easy as picking a daisy. They entered what looked like a Tommy Bahama furniture catalog. A dark mahogany bar, the expanse of the back wall, with a background of floor to ceiling windows; the room was wide open with dark leather couches, eight pseudo palm trees scattered around, huge paddleboard ceiling fans, and a pool table off to the side. They headed upstairs to four bedrooms, which, again, Rosalie had nailed, each with their own private bathroom. After surveying the entire floor, they headed back downstairs. Leanne curious as to where the kitchen was, walked over to a huge sliding mahogany door. She gave it a little push and it slid open to expose an industrial size kitchen with stainless steel counter tops and appliances. The cabinets looked like bamboo, but the showcase was the huge ten-seater island in the middle. She slowly entered the kitchen and said, "Holy shit. I think I died and went to heaven."

Devon, standing two feet behind her, casually said, "I wouldn't mind seeing you whip up some of your berry delights in here."

Rosalie rolled her eyes and said, "Forget about her berries, Romeo, look at what you are going to own. Chet's right, it's like a hotel."

That brought them all back to reality.

Leanne ran her hand along the island. She turned and locked eyes with Devon and said, "Devon, let me ask you a question. Why are you buying this house?"

Devon held her gaze and replied, "Because I've decided to make all of you my family, considering I don't have any."

Leanne teared up. Unable to respond, just nodded.

Amber came around from behind Devon and said, "Well, I, for one, would love to have you as part of my family. That goes for all of you. Heck, what's five more added to the clan I already have."

Leonard put his arm around her shoulder and agreed.

Rosalie, not good with emotional baggage, said, "Yeah, well, considering I don't have any either, or any to speak of really, I guess I could use a brother."

She winked at Devon.

Chet, standing quietly behind the other's, cleared his throat and said, "Well, I'm figuring it's about time to get a move on."

Devon turned to him and said, "Not so fast there, my friend. You're part of this clan now and there's something I would like you to think about."

Chet, not very comfortable with five pairs of eyes staring at him, said, "Well, I guess I could do that, considering I got a brain."

That sent a chuckle through the room.

Devon walked over to Chet and put a hand on his shoulder, and said, "How do you feel about moving to the island with me? I won't be here all of the time, but it would be nice to have someone looking out for the place. And when I am, it would be nice to have your company and the hounds, of course."

At this point, there wasn't a dry eye in the house, literally. Chet cleared his throat of the tears that clogged it and said, "I might be willing to give that some thought."

Devon, feeling the emotions well up in him, said, "I could sure use a man like you in my life."

He pulled Chet in for a hug. After a few seconds of composing himself, Devon stepped back and said, "Okay, let's see if we can find some house keys, considering I won't have Boy Wonder here to pick the locks for me, then we can head to the mainland."

The others, still unable to speak, just nodded, and they headed back to the main house.

They searched the kitchen, and as luck would have it, they found numerous keys in one of the kitchen draws. Devon grabbed all of them and headed to the front door. After trying three keys with no luck, he finally found the correct one on the fourth try. He went back to the kitchen and told the others to go out the front door. He would lock up the back doors and be right out. Once he secured the doors and turned off the lights, he joined the others. He met them on the porch and said, "Now, let's go find that golf cart."

They headed around to the back of the house.

Leonard spotted a storage shed on the left, past the pool house and said, "My money's on that shed over there."

All eyes followed his pointing arm and agreed. They walked over to the shed. Devon undid the latch and slid the door open. There sat a shiny eight-seater custom golf cart.

Chet said, "Bingo. Now, find which one of them keys fits."

Devon walked over and tried the rest of the keys in his hand; none belonged to the cart.

Leanne walked over and said, "Let me take a look. If there's one thing I know, its golf carts."

Amber asked, "How do you know about golf carts, Leanne?

Leanne, running her hand under the seat, felt the key, and brought it out. She turned and dangled it in front of the others and said, "Because I'm married to a lawyer. He has a custom cart he keeps in our garage. The kids would beg him to take them for a ride, but he always said, "Not now, I'm busy." So, one day, after searching inside for the key, I went out to the golf cart and did the exact same thing I just did here, and found the key. I loaded the kids up in it and we went for a ride all around the neighborhood. We had a blast."

"Okay, hop in everyone," Chet gave a loud whistle and the hounds came running and jumped on the back.

She drove it around to the slope and stopped, "Um, I don't think this will make it up the hill."

They looked around and Leonard pointed out a path 20 yards to the left. Leanne backed it up and turned toward the clearing. She turned into the woods and found the path leading back to the beach, and they headed for Sadie.

Thirty minutes later, they were parked next to the dock. Everyone got out, but Devon. Leanne looked at him and said, "I'll go park this up in the woods a bit and meet you at the plane."

Devon stayed seated and replied, "I'll come with you, so I know where it is when I return in a few days."

Leanne nodded and drove up the path toward the cabin. They drove for five minutes, found a spot in the brush, and parked it.

Leanne turned to Devon and said, "This runs on a battery. You'll have to charge it when you get it back to the house."

Devon looked at her and tucked a strand of loose hair behind her ear, and said, "I'll be back on Monday, so it should be fine till then."

Leanne nodded and turned to get out of the cart, but Devon gently grabbed her arm and said, "I need a minute of your time, alone."

Feeling butterflies having a parade in her belly, Leanne said, "Okay."

She sat back down.

Devon started, "Well, I wanted to explain my decision to buy the house."

Leanne held up a hand and said, "You don't need to explain to me."

Devon reached out and held her hand and replied, "Yes, I do. But, for now, I will only give you one of the reasons."

Curious, Leanne raised an eyebrow and said, "Okay, go on. I'm listening."

Devon adjusted his position to face her and said, "Um, well, I was thinking it might be nice to have Amber and Leonard's wedding here on the island, being that this is where their story began."

Astonished, Leanne asked, "At the cabin?"

Devon laughed and said, "No, silly. I was thinking at the big house. There's plenty of room to put up that large clan of hers and I thought it would be a nice location; being that they agree, that is."

A slow smile crept across Leanne's face, and she finally said, "Well, Romeo, aren't you just full of surprises. I think it's a wonderful idea and I'm sure Amber and Leonard will think so, too."

Relieved, Devon reluctantly let go of Leanne's hand and said, "All righty, then. Let's go ask the lovebirds."

They climbed out of the golf cart. Leanne tossed Devon the keys, and they headed down the path to the beach.

Leanne and Devon walked down the dock to where the others were standing. With everyone together, Chet said, "Okay, folks. Let's get this show on the road."

Leanne nudged Devon, who cleared his throat and said, "Um, well, Chet, I need just another minute."

He turned to Amber and Leonard and said, "Amber, Leonard, I was wondering if you would be interested in having your wedding here on Welby Island..."

He barely got the words out of his mouth before Amber squealed, and came barreling at him, arms wide open. She tackled him, and before he knew what hit him, they both went flying off the edge of the dock into the Puget Sound. The others ran to the edge of the dock, and two seconds later, Blaze and Bella leaped into the water.

Laughing, Rosalie said, "Boy Wonder, go rescue her."

Leonard didn't hesitate one second, and jumped right in.

Leanne looked at Rosalie and said, "Well?"

Rosalie grabbed Leanne's hand and off the dock they went.

Ten minutes later, all five of them, soaking wet, plus the two hounds, walked back up the dock to where Chet was standing with his hands on his hips. He looked them over and said, "What in tarnation was that all about?"

Feeling like scolded children, they just shrugged. Chet opened the hatch on Sadie and brought out a pile of towels and handed one to each of them. Trying not to let the laugh he was holding in escape, he said, "So, that's what I been missing all these years without kids. Lordy, my Annie, she would of been right there in that Sound with you."

The clan broke down in laughter.

They dried off and boarded the plane. Rosalie took the seat next to Chet since Leonard and Amber were snuggled up together in the back of the plane and Devon claimed the seat next to Leanne. Once Chet got Sadie airborne, Leanne said to Devon, "I guess from Amber's reaction, her answer is yes to holding the wedding on the island."

Devon replied, "Oh, yes, and she almost bloody drowned me in the process."

Leanne laughed and said, "Good thing it's only a 20-minute flight, considering we all look like drowned rats."

Devon turned and looked at Leanne, and said, "Well, if that's the case, you're the most gorgeous drowned rat I've ever laid eyes on."

Flustered, Leanne turned and looked out the window, as her heart skipped a beat.

Chapter 32

Chet landed Sadie at the dock in Seattle. Once he was secured by the dock crew, he unbuckled his seat belt, turned to the others, and announced, "Okay, folks. Here we are."

He got up, unlatched the door, and climbed out.

Rosalie followed him, handed him her bag as he helped her down. Once her feet were on solid ground, she declared, "Damn, it feels good to be back in civilization."

Devon came off next. He turned and held out a hand to Leanne to help her off. Leonard was next, lifted Amber off by the waist, twirling her in a circle. Once everybody was on the dock, Chet asked, "So, folks, what's your plan from here?"

Devon took out his cell phone and replied, "I know of a hotel nearby. I'll call and make reservations for the night."

Chet looked at the others and said, "I'm betting you're all happier than a sack of clams to be off that island."

Rosalie was the only one to respond, "Oh boy, am I."

Devon hung up the phone, turned to the group, and said, "Okay, I have us booked at the Tremont. They're sending the hotel shuttle for us."

Chet took off his cap, ran his fingers through his hair, and said, "Well then, I guess me and the hounds ought to be heading on home."

Devon asked Chet, "Do you have a car here?"

Chet replied, "Yup, got my pick up right over there."

Amber, kneeling on the dock petting Blaze and Bella, asked Chet, "How far do you live from here?"

Chet replied, "Not far. I'm just a mile up the road there."

Devon asked Chet for his cell phone number. Chet chuckled and said, "Son, I don't got one of those fangled phones, but I got a land line you can reach me on."

He gave Devon the number.

Shocked, Leonard said to Chet, "What! How can you not have a cell phone? You're flying all over the place. You live alone, and you go hiking with the hounds. You need a cell phone in case of an emergency!"

Chet pat Leonard's shoulder and said, "My boy, I'm old school. I wouldn't know what to do with one of them cellular phones, anyhow."

All eyes shot to Devon. He laughed and said, "I'm on it."

The hotel shuttle pulled into the parking lot. The driver hopped out, and started loading their bags.

Amber walked over and hugged Chet, and said, "I'm going to miss you. Leonard and I were talking on the flight over here and decided we would like to get married on Welby Island Labor Day Weekend, if that's okay with ya'll."

Devon stepped forward and put his arm around Amber's shoulder, and said, "That sounds perfect. Does that work for the rest of you?"

Rosalie, Leanne, and Chet nodded.

Chet removed his cap, and asked Amber, "Country Girl, I was wondering, seeing that I'm a Justice of the Peace, and if it's okay with you and Leonard, I would like to do the honor of marrying you two."

Thank goodness they were nowhere near the edge of the dock, because Amber squealed and flew at Chet, wrapping her arms around his neck, jumping up and down, and said, "Yes! Yes! That would make our wedding day perfect! Oh, thank you, Chet!"

Leonard walked over to Amber and Chet and wrapped his arms around both of them, and said, "Thank you, Chet."

Leanne and Rosalie wiped their tears away and walked over, and hugged the group. Devon cleared his throat and said, "Well, okay then, it's settled. Labor Day Weekend is three months from now, and we will all be together again on Welby Island for the wedding of Boy Wonder and Country Girl."

They said their goodbyes to Chet, climbed into the waiting van, and drove off.

Chapter 33
Three months later
Amber and Leonard's Wedding

Thursday morning, Chet and Devon were having coffee at the kitchen table. Chet got up and put his coffee mug in the sink, turned to Devon, and said, "I got some errands to run on the mainland. While I'm there, I'll check up on those caters, see if everything is in order for Saturday's nuptials."

Devon replied, "That would be great. Can you also check with the harbormaster to make sure the boat I charted to bring the guest out to the island tomorrow is all set?"

Chet grabbed his cap and said, "Sure thing. Henry and I go way back. And ever since you bought me that fancy schmancy boat to go to and from with, he's your biggest fan. He'll do right by you, don't you worry about nothing. I'm leaving Bella and Blaze here with you. They get one whiff of whatever is cooking at the caterer, ain't telling what might happen. I reckon I won't be more than a couple of hours."

Devon nodded and said, "Take your time. And for the love of the Queen, no speeding in that fancy schmancy boat of yours."

Chet laughed and walked out of the kitchen toward the front door.

* * *

Devon was sitting on the front porch, playing his guitar, working on a new song, when he spotted Chet's boat pulling up to the dock. Blaze and Bella, who were lying at his feet, stood up, raced down the stairs, and across the lawn to greet Chet. They were barking and jumping with excitement, tails wagging wildly. It was then, that Devon saw the reason for all the excitement; Chet was lifting not one, but two, small children off the boat. Devon slowly stood and watched as Chet helped Leanne off the boat. A slow, wide grin, spread across his face. He headed down the stairs and across the lawn at a leisurely pace, taking in the scene in front of him. The two kids, who were followed closely by Blaze and Bella, were running down the dock towards him, laughing, and the hounds barking. When Devon reached them, he said, "Well, who do we have here?"

Luke looked up at him and said, "I'm Luke and this is my sister, Lindsey. We're twins."

Devon smiled and said, "Ah, yes. I believe I have heard about you two."

Just then, Chet and Leanne approached. Devon and Leanne locked eyes. Holding it until Lindsey, pulling on Devon's shorts, said, "Are you Mommy's friend, Devon? Are you really a Rock Star?"

Devon smiled and replied, "Well, yes, that would be me and yes, I dabble in music now and again."

Luke looked at Devon and said, "You talk funny."

That brought a round of laughter from the adults.

Leanne decided to bring this inquisition to a halt. She said, "Lindsey, Luke, this is my friend Devon I told you about. He lives, here, on the island."

Confused, Luke said, "You live on this island all by yourself, did you buy it?

Devon smiled and said, "As a matter of fact, I do, and I did. However, Mr. Chet, Bella, and Blaze live here with me."

Stunned, Leanne looked at Devon and said, "You bought the whole island?"

Devon looked at her with a sly grin and replied, "Well, yes, it sort of came with the house."

Listening, Luke turned to his mother and said, "Wow! Mommy, can we live on this island instead of our new house?"

Leanne, not yet fully recovered from hearing that Devon now owned Welby Island, said, "No. But it's only a short boat ride from our new house. I'm sure Devon wouldn't mind if we visited every once in a while."

Luke responded, "Cool!"

Devon turned to Leanne, raised an eyebrow and said, "A, short boat ride away, are you now?"

Leanne didn't want to get into all the nitty gritty details in front of the kids, so she replied, "Um, yes, we…"

That is when Lindsey interrupted and said, "Yup. We divorced Daddy because he was banging Allie, our nanny. So, now, we live in Seattle."

Chet cleared his throat and said, "You kids want to go meet Sadie?"

Lindsey laughed and said to Leanne, "Mr. Chet named his plane Sadie. Isn't that silly?"

Then Luke asked, "Mommy, can we?"

Grateful for Chet's distraction, she said, "Sure, but stick close to Mr. Chet and behave."

Luke grabbed Lindsey's hand and said, "We will."

And they ran off with Chet, with Bella and Blaze close behind.

Leanne stared after them for a minute. She turned and looked at Devon, who now had both eyebrows raised, "Well, well, Queen Bee, aren't you just full of surprises."

Leanne, looking at the ground, shuffled her feet, and replied, "Um, well, I guess after walking into your own home to find your husband banging the nanny, whom he hired the minute I left for the airport. Not much more can surprise me."

Devon took a step closer to Leanne, put a finger under her chin and lifted it so she was looking at him, and said, "We'll get to that. But for now, what do you say we bring your bags up to the house."

Leanne nodded and turned to look at the kids. Devon put an arm around her shoulders and said, "They're fine. Chet will keep an eye on them."

Leanne smiled and said, "I know. I just love seeing them this happy, and Chet, too."

Devon agreed and they headed across the lawn to the house.

Chapter 34

Devon, Chet, Leanne, and the kids spent the afternoon lounging by the pool. Luke and Lindsey found it hysterical that the hounds would jump into the pool right after them, which was a great source of entertainment. By five o'clock, the kids and hounds were tuckered out. So, they went into the pool house to watch T.V.

Leanne, sitting on the patio with Chet and Devon, said, "I, still, can't get over the fact that the fake gurus had satellite communication on the island, but we didn't get a signal."

Devon replied, "We didn't get a signal because we were buried back in the woods, and when we found their hidey hole, we didn't give it much thought."

Chet piped in and said, "And those Claines, they be telling me that they were staying on the mainland. My Annie, sharp as a tack she was, she would have been on to them faster than a scurrying cockroach."

Chet's analogy made Devon and Leanne laugh.

Chet pushed up out of his chair and said, "Well, I better tend to those steaks. When those little ones get restless, they'll be hungrier than a stray hound; after all that fun they had in the pool."

Leanne looked at Devon with questioning eyes, which in turn, Devon said, "Turns out Chet, here, knows his way around the kitchen. And considering we don't have any take away places on the island, I'm happy to let him have at it."

Leanne stood and said, "Chet, can I give you hand with anything?"

Chet replied, "Well, I wouldn't mind much if you put together a salad of sorts."

Devon stood and said, "Well, I just happen to have two hands, also. What can I do?"

"Nothing," responded Leanne and Chet at the same time, which set them off into a fit of laughter.

"Oh, aren't you two a funny pair," mumbled Devon, as he followed them into the house.

Leanne cleaned the lettuce and chopped veggies for the salad. Then went into the pantry, which was bigger than the master bedroom closet, she grabbed a bottle of olive oil and balsamic vinegar to make a dressing for the salad. She sat down at the kitchen island and began whisking the ingredients together.

Devon sat down next to her and handed her a glass of Chardonnay. She looked over at him, smiled, and said, "Thank you."

Devon turned to Chet, and asked, "Chet, can I pour you a glass of red wine?"

Chet turned, wiped his hands on the dish towel, and said, "No, but I wouldn't mind one of those fancy beers you have there in the icebox."

Devon stood to get the beer. Chet walked over to Leanne and leaned on the island, and said to her, "That boy, there, keeps trying to get me to drink that red wine. He keeps telling me it's good for my heart, and I keep telling him my hearts just fine; ticking away like a clock, red meat, cold beer, and the occasional cigar, keeps me fit as a fiddle."

Surprised, Leanne asked, "You smoke cigars?"

Chet took a sip of the beer Devon placed in front of him and replied, "Now and again at my monthly poker game, or when me and the fellas are out fishing."

Leanne turned to Devon wide eyed, who in turn said, "Oh yes. Our Chet, here, has quite the active social agenda, and a group of cronies he hangs out with."

Chet laughed and said, "Aw, you're just still sore because they beat the knickers off of you last Tuesday night, took him for 80 bucks."

Leanne picked up her glass of wine and took a sip, smiled at Devon, and said, "Is that right?"

Devon shot Chet the evil eye, which only set Chet off into a fit of laughter. Devon said to Chet humorously, "Oh, you think it's funny, do you. Well, I'll fix those cronies next time."

"Next time?" asked Leanne.

Devon took a sip of his wine and replied, "Well, Chet here has quite the schedule; Monday nights, he meets the cronies at a pub by the harbor to watch baseball or whatever bloody sport they can find. Thursday mornings, at the ungodly hour of four a.m., he goes over and picks up those same cronies, and they go fishing for half the bloody day."

Chet laughed and said, "Still stinging from not catching nothing, are ya?"

Surprised, Leanne turned to Devon, and asked, "You went fishing with them?"

Devon replied, "Yes, and it's the last bloody time I'll do that. They're worse than you cackling hens."

Leanne laughed, turned to Chet, and asked, "You don't come home late at night on the boat or Sadie, do you?"

Chet took a swig of his beer and said, "Naw. I still got my trailer back on the mainland and I keep my truck parked at the marina."

Relieved, Leanne said, "Good. Because if Amber caught wind of this, she would kick Devon's ass."

Just then, the twins and hounds came barreling into the kitchen. Lindsey ran up to Leanne and said, "We're hungry."

Leanne handed them each a few pieces of cucumber and said, "Eat these, and then go get out of your swim suits. Dinner will be ready in a little bit."

In unison, they both said, "Okay, Mommy."

The twins ran off down the hallway with Blaze and Bella on their heels.

Chet set down his beer and said, "I better go fire up the grill. Those little ones will be chompin' at the bit before long."

Leaving Leanne and Devon alone, Leanne got up, and started fidgeting around the kitchen. Devon watched her for a few minutes with amusement, and finally said, "Leanne."

She took a deep breath and slowly turned around and said, "Devon."

Devon smiled and said, "You're fidgeting."

Flustered, Leanne said, "I am not fidgeting. I'm just putting a few things away."

Devon got up and walked towards her. Leanne backed up. He took another step closer and she backed up right into the refrigerator. With nowhere left to go, she looked up at Devon, and what she saw in his eyes made her insides do flips. He reached out and tucked a strand of hair behind her ear. She was paralyzed; couldn't move, couldn't breathe. Just as he was leaning in to kiss her, the kids and hounds came clattering down the stairs. Leanne quickly pushed Devon away, but not before he tapped her nose and said, "To be continued."

He turned towards the kids as they raced into the kitchen.

He grabbed Luke around the waist and swung him into the air, then set him on the ground. Lindsey, pulling on Devon's shorts, squealed, "My turn. Do it to me. Do it to me!"

Leanne touched her sizzling nose and said to herself, *Oh boy.*

She turned to watch Devon and her kids laughing and twirling.

Chet walked into the kitchen and said, "Got her going. Needs another 30 minutes to get good and hot, then it'll be ready for them steaks."

Leanne turned to Devon and the kids and said, "Let's take this out back. You guys can throw a ball to Blaze and Bella."

Hearing their names, the two hounds ran to the back door wagging their tails. Devon opened the door and they all ran out laughing and barking.

Leanne went to the refrigerator and grabbed a beer for Chet; opened it and handed it to him. She picked up the two wine glasses and said, "Let's go sit outside and watch the kids, including the big one."

Chet took a sip of his beer and said to Leanne, "He's a good man, Leanne; got a heart the size of this here country. And he's got it something bad for you. This probably ain't my place to say, but because I'm mighty fond of both of you, I'm hoping it might be a two way lane, if you know what I mean."

Knowing exactly what he meant, Leanne said, "I think it's heading that way, but I needed to figure things out. That's why I didn't contact him when I got to Seattle last month. I needed time with Luke and Lindsey. They've had a lot to adjust to these past months; with me being away, then the divorce, plus, our move to Seattle. I had to make them my main focus."

Chet nodded and said, "Them is two great kids you got there. And you being the good momma that you are, I reckon it will all work out."

Leanne smiled, walked over to Chet, kissed his cheek, and said, "Me, too."

They headed outside.

Winded, Devon plopped down in the chair next to Leanne and said, "Queen Bee, I can see now why you were drop dead exhausted by the day's end. Those two wear you to the bone."

Leanne laughed and said, "Oh, you haven't seen anything yet."

Chet got up to poke the fire, and Leanne screeched, "Oh my God!"

Chet jumped back and said, "What the heck! What are you squawking about, Leanne?"

Leanne jumped up out of her chair and ran over to the grill. She turned to Devon, with tears in her eyes, and said, "You brought it here."

Devon smiled and said, "Well, of course, I did."

Chet, still trying to slow his heart rate down, said, "Brought what here? What is wrong with you two?"

Leanne touched Chet's arm and said, "I'm sorry I startled you."

Chet, with his hand on his heart, said, "Startled? You damn near knocked the ticker right out of me. I might need that red wine after all."

Devon, having tried to contain his laughter, just lost it. When he finally calmed down, he said to Chet, "Welcome to my world, mate. Believe me when I tell you, when Rosalie and Amber get here, you will be guzzling red wine straight from the bottle."

Leanne apologized to Chet again, and explained how Leonard built the grill from junk he found in the garage at the cabin.

Chet, with a regular heartbeat now, said, "I'm gonna go in and get those steaks. You ain't gonna be screechin' and hollerin' when I put them on that there grill, are you?"

Leanne went and sat back down at the table where Devon was still chuckling. Ten minutes later, Chet called to the kids and hounds, "Chow time."

They all came running.

* * *

Leanne put down her fork, sat back, and said to Chet, "That was delicious. What did you put on those steaks?"

Chet wiped his mouth and replied, "My Annie, she was the cook in the kitchen. Me; all I could do was barbeque. I just rubbed them with a clove of garlic and then sprinkle on some salt and pepper, nothing much to it."

Leanne stared at Chet, and then looked at Devon, who was smiling from ear to ear, and asked, "Did you tell him?"

Devon raised both hands in the air and replied, "No, I swear. The first time he did it, it took all of my willpower not to call you."

Chet, lost in the conversation, asked, "What I miss?"

Leanne laughed and said, "Remember those steaks you put in our second food delivery?"

Chet nodded and said, "Yup, picked them up at Pete's; freshest meat in Seattle."

Leanne continued, "Well, after we spent the day painting our dictionary of feelings on the cabin..."

Luke interrupted and said, "Mommy, you painted words on a cabin. Is that, like, a house?"

Devon looked at Leanne with raised eyebrows. Leanne turned to Luke and said, "Well, yes, honey. We all did. It's kind of like when your teacher, Ms. Rosa, asked you to go to the blackboard and spell a word."

Luke nodded in understanding.

Leanne continued telling Chet the story, "So, anyway, we decided to reward ourselves by having a barbeque using that very grill you used tonight that Leonard made."

Chet, fully recovered, said, "So that's what set you screeching like a seagull."

Leanne smiled and said, "Yes. But, the point is we had the barbeque after the last visit from the gurus..."

"What's a guru?" Lindsey asked.

Trying not to give the little ears too much information about her stay at Claine cabin, Leanne replied, "Um, well, a guru is someone who knows a lot about different things."

Chet and Devon both with their mouths full, said, "Hmm."

Leanne ignored them and continued her story, "So, anyway, I prepared the steaks. And, after we ate, Devon complimented me on them. I told him that I didn't do anything special; just

165

rubbed them with garlic cloves and sprinkled them with salt and pepper, so when you said you did the same, I thought he showed you how to do it."

Chet smiled and said, "Nope, young lady. I've been doing them that way for going on 30 years now. I haven't done it once since my Annie passed on, but figuring I got some extended family now, I gotta step up to the plate."

Leanne reached over and took Chet's hand, and said, "Well, we appreciate it."

Luke and Lindsey both added, "Mr. Chet, that was really yummy."

When everyone finished eating, Leanne turned to the twins, and said, "It's bath time and bed for you two. We have a really big day ahead of us tomorrow. So, go on up and pick out your jammies, I'll be up in a minute to run your bath."

Both kids hopped off their chairs and went over to Chet and hugged him, and said, "Thank you, Mr. Chet, for the yummy dinner."

Glassy eyed, Chet bent down and wrapped his arms around them, and said, "Go on now, get some sleep. Tomorrow, I got some big plans for us; I thought we might go down to the beach and catch us some crabs."

The two kids squealed with delight. As they were heading out of the kitchen, they turned back and ran over to Devon and gave him a big hug. Then, they ran off giggling with the hounds right behind them.

Chet cleared his throat and said to Leanne and Devon, "If you don't mind, I think I'll go find one of them bloody hell sports on T.V that Devon is so fond of."

Leanne got up to start clearing the table, Devon put a hand on her arm and said, "I got it, Queen Bee. It seems Chet and I have the same arrangement as you and I did at the cabin; he cooks, I clean. Go tend to the kids. When they are fast asleep, come meet me on the front porch. I want to talk to you."

Leanne held his gaze and said, "Okay."

* * *

An hour later, Leanne walked out onto the front porch and found Devon strumming on his guitar. She walked over and sat down in the rocking chair next to him, and quietly asked, "Is that a new song you're working on?"

Devon put the guitar down by the side of his chair and replied, "Actually, I've been working on it for some time now, just needs an ending."

Leanne nodded as she was staring out at the water. After a few minutes, Devon broke the silence and quietly said, "I'm glad you're here."

Leanne didn't turn to look at him, but replied, "Me, too."

Not knowing where to go with the here and now, she decided to focus on tomorrow. Turning to Devon, she asked, "So when is everyone else arriving?"

Devon replied, "I believe the circus is arriving sometime around two p.m."

Leanne laughed and said, "The circus, huh? How many people are in that circus?"

Devon counted on his fingers, "Well, we have the Quinn clan that consists of Amber, Momma, Daddy, sister Hannah, husband Clay, Clay Jr. Mikey, Quentin, and the new arrival, baby Claire. Then we have Brother Bailey Jr., wife Jenna and their two kids; Brandon and Becky, Petey, the high school star quarterback. Not sure if Brother Ted is going to make it from Germany. Then we have Leonard, Mr. and Mrs. Mathers, grandparents Sylvia and Charles Mathers, Rosalie, Chet, you, and the twins and me; that brings the circus total to 25."

Leanne laughed and said, "How in the world did you remember all of those names?"

Devon, in all seriousness, said, "Oh, I've been studying. And don't you worry. I made us some cheat sheets."

Leanne laughed and said, "Good thing, because I'm going to need one. Have you decided where you are going to put everyone?"

Devon smiled and replied, "Well, it just so happens, that our mystery man, Chet, is quite the popular chap back on the mainland and has a friend that works in one of the hotels over there, whom he brought to the island to tend to all of the arrangements. We have Bailey Jr. and Hannah's clan in the north wing, along with Petey. Momma and Daddy are in the main house with us, as is Rosalie. The Mathers and grands are in the pool house.

Leanne did the math, then turned to Devon, and asked, "Um, where are the newlyweds staying?"

Devon had been waiting for her to ask that question. He smiled and said, "Well, they have requested the honeymoon suite, of course."

Leanne eyed him, and asked, "Where, exactly, is the honeymoon suite, Devon?"

He sat forward and replied, "The cabin. They'll stay somewhere here tomorrow night. Then, they want to stay there Saturday night after the wedding and Sunday night before they head off on their true honeymoon Monday morning."

Leanne stared at him and said, "You have got to be kidding me."

Devon shook his head and said, "Nope, and as a matter of fact, that is one of the things I wanted to talk to you about."

Skeptical, Leanne said, "Really?"

Devon, not sure how to approach this, decided head on would be best, "Um, well, yes. It was a special request from the bride to be. So, I was thinking that, maybe, you and I could take a golf cart ride over there tomorrow morning and add a few finishing touches. Chet's gal has already done the linens and such, but I thought a few extra touches were in order."

Still staring at him dead on, Leanne said, "Such as?"

Devon squirmed in his seat a bit and replied, "Um, well, I was thinking maybe a chilled bottle of French champagne, a dozen chocolate covered strawberries, perhaps."

Leanne continued to stare at Devon, and then slowly, like the sun setting into the water, a smile appeared on her face, and she said, "Rock Star, you never cease to amaze me. Do you think we could hijack a couple of the pool lounge chairs and set them up on the beach for the happy couple?"

Relieved, Devon replied, "I like the way you think, Locomotive."

They hashed out the details for another half hour, then Leanne yawned and said, "What time were you thinking of heading over there?"

"What time do the twins wake?" asked Devon.

Leanne laughed and said, "Oh, you don't want to know."

Devon put his face in his hands and said, "Oh bloody hell, tell me."

168

Leanne giggled and said, "Around seven. But, after today, they could sleep until noon."

Devon lifted his head and said, "Oh, okay, that's not so terrible. What do you say we head out around nine?"

"Perfect," said Leanne.

Devon added, "Chet promised them crabbing, so we can take advantage of that, and then be back in time to meet the caterer, who is going to set up for the night's festivities and the wedding on Saturday."

Curious, Leanne asked, "What's on the agenda for the night's festivities?"

Devon smiled and replied, "I had in mind an authentic New Orleans crawfish dinner."

Leanne smiled right back at him and said, "You've thought of everything, haven't you? They will be thrilled."

Devon stood, held out a hand to Leanne, and said, "And then some."

Leanne helped Devon lock up the house and turn off all the lights, and headed upstairs. They both looked in on the twins and found them fast asleep, each with a hound tucked snuggly next to them. Leanne quietly closed the door, crossed the hall to her room. With her hand on the knob, she turned to Devon, and said, "Thank you for everything. Thank you for having us, and thank you for being so kind to my children."

Devon, leaning on the opposite wall, said, "It's easy, Queen Bee. Like I said, I'm happy you're here."

Leanne smiled and said, "Good night, Devon."

Devon replied, "Good night, Leanne."

He walked down the hall to his room.

Chapter 35

The following morning Leanne woke up to bright sunshine and chirping birds. She looked at the clock by her bedside and said, "Oh shit."

She jumped out of bed, hurried into the bathroom, cursing herself for sleeping until eight. She pulled a pair of shorts and a tank top out of her bag, threw them on and grabbed her ratty sneakers, and took off downstairs. When she got to the kitchen, she stopped dead in her tracks. Devon was at the stove, flipping pancakes, Chet was pouring juice into glasses for the twins, who were yapping a million miles a minute. Smiling, Leanne moved forward into the kitchen and, the twins squealed, "Hi Mommy! Devon's making us pancakes and Mr. Chet made us juice from real oranges."

Leanne responded, "Well, I can see that."

She walked over and gave them each a kiss on the head. She turned to Chet and said, "Good morning, Chet."

He smiled over at her and said, "Morning, Leanne. There's coffee over there in the pot, why don't you get a cup and come sit down."

Leanne looked over at Devon as he plated the pancakes, and asked, "What can I do to help?"

Devon walked over and put the plates down in front of the kids and replied, "Nothing at all. Chet and I have it all under control."

She poured herself a cup of coffee and sat down at the island counter. Devon put a plate of pancakes in front of her. She looked at them, then looked at Devon, and said, "Mickey Mouse pancakes?"

Lindsey, bursting with delight, said, "Look, Mommy, Devon made mine into Minnie Mouse. He gave her a bow with the syrup."

Luke chimed in. "And he made a face on mine. I'm going to eat Mickey's ears first," he said picking up the whole pancake and bit off Mickey's ear.

Leanne laughed and said, "Would you like me to cut them up for you?"

Luke shook his head and said, "No, it's funner this way."

Lindsey added, "Yeah, it's funner to eat them whole, that's what Devon said."

Leanne turned to Devon and raised an eyebrow at him. He just smiled and shrugged.

When the twins were done eating, Chet clapped his hands and said, "Okay, youngins', let's get this show on the road. Those crabs ain't gonna wait all day to meet ya."

Luke and Lindsey hopped off their stool, turned to Devon, and said, "Thanks for the pancakes, Devon."

The twins ran out of the kitchen straight for the front door; the hounds right behind them.

Chet turned to Leanne and said, "They'll be good with me. Why don't you two be on your way?"

Grateful, Leanne said, "Thank you, Chet."

She stood up and kissed his cheek.

He looked at her and said, "Hell, they keep me young, it's my pleasure."

And, off he went after the kids and hounds.

Leanne turned, looked at Devon, and said, "What in the world. I never even heard them wake."

Devon leaned against the counter and said, "Well, that might be because they decided it would be more fun to come wake me at the crack of dawn. There I was, soundly sleeping, next thing I know I have four tiny hands tickling me, and jumping up and down on the bed."

Astonished, Leanne said, "Oh my God! Devon, I am so sorry."

Devon finished off his coffee and said, "Don't fret, Queen Bee. I loved every minute of it."

Leanne, not sure what just happened, but it felt like her whole body bloomed like a rose. She felt heat from her head to her toes. She got up and placed her coffee cup in the sink, then walked over to Devon, stood on her tippy toes and kissed his cheek, and said with tears in her eyes, "Thank you."

171

Devon doing everything in his power to not swoop her off her feet and carry her upstairs and make wild passionate love to her, took a step back, and said, "Um, your welcome."

Leanne turned back to the island and began gathering the breakfast dishes, brought them to the sink, rinsed them, and loaded them into the dishwasher. She gathered the pans and bowls off the counter, and did the same with them.

Devon, having pulled himself together, cleared his throat and said, "I'll go see about loading a couple of those lounge chairs onto the golf cart. Could you grab the bag in the refrigerator with the champagne and strawberries on your way out? I'll meet you out back."

Leanne smiled and said, "Sure, I'll be out in a few minutes."

Ten minutes later, they had the golf cart loaded and were on their way. Neither one of them spoke a word, until they reached the beach where it all began. They jumped out of the cart and unloaded the lounge chairs. They decided to put them down by the water, near the cove they had once fished in. They got back in the cart and took the path that led to Claine Cabin. As they emerged from the woods, Leanne put her hands to her mouth, and tears rolled down her cheeks. Devon parked the cart near the back porch, turned to Leanne, and saw that she was crying. He got out of the cart and walked around to her side, and held out a hand to her. She took his hand and slowly got out of the cart.

Devon wrapped his arm around her shoulders, kissed her head, and said, "It got to me too, the first time I came back. I can't explain the feeling, except it wasn't one of misery. It was more like I'd come home to a place I missed."

Leanne, unable to speak, just nodded.

They stood there for a few minutes just staring at the cabin, then Leanne took a deep breath, wiped the tears from her cheeks, and said, "I'm okay, let's go in."

Devon reached into the golf cart and grabbed the bag with the champagne and strawberries and handed it to Leanne. He turned back and took out another bag packed with beach towels and sun lotions. They headed up the back stairs and Devon held the door open for Leanne. Once inside the kitchen, Leanne's eyes canvassed the room and all the memories created there came rushing back.

Devon took the champagne and strawberries out of the bag, walked over, and put them in the refrigerator. When he closed the door, he found Leanne standing in front of him. They locked eyes and held them until Devon leaned down and kissed her. They kissed slowly and passionately, until Leanne began pulling Devon's shirt up and over his head; standing still as a statue. When he could finally move, he lifted Leanne's tank top up and off. He kissed her again, but this time, with lust and want. They circled the kitchen, lips locked together, ending up on the floor, naked.

Devon on his back with Leanne collapsed on his chest, said breathlessly, "Buggers, we just christened the cabin before the newlyweds."

Leanne laughed and said, "I've wanted to roll around on this kitchen floor with you since day one."

Regaining some of his oxygen, Devon replied, "I hardly believe since day one. As I recall, we didn't quite like each other very much, when we first met."

Leanne agreed and said, "You're right. It must have been when I got zapped by the toaster."

Devon lifted Leanne's head and said seriously, "I never zapped you with a toaster."

Leanne laughed, rolled off Devon, sat up, and said, "I know you didn't. But, remember the time you came into the kitchen and scared me half to death?"

Devon laughed, "Yes, I remember that quite clearly. You had batter on your face and I wiped it off."

Excitedly, Leanne said, "Yes! When your finger touched my face, I got what felt like an electric shock."

Devon smiled and said, "Hence, like being zapped by a toaster."

Pleased, Leanne said, "Exactly!"

Devon sat up and faced Leanne, and said, "The first time I wanted to roll around on this kitchen floor with you was the night we called a truce after Blair and Micah came for dinner and Boy Wonder blew them out of the water with his tale of how we divvied up the chore list with a game of strip poker. You and I had a little tiff earlier on about me swiping a piece of bread. We said a few nasty things to one another, and when you apologized later that evening, as did I, I knew then that you were the kind of woman I had always been looking for, but never found. One who could laugh, cry, fight, forgive, and, most importantly, love. I wondered to myself, even knowing that you were married, that if one day you would be able to love me and spend the rest of our lives together."

Leanne leaned forward, kissed Devon, and said, "As you know, I returned home to find my husband banging the nanny he hired three minutes after I left on my journey to enlightenment; which he implored I go to, if I wanted to save our marriage. Well, come to find out during the divorce proceedings, he has been banging everyone from his secretary, divorcee' clients, to the wife of the golf pro at the country club, among others; all beginning right after our 'I do's' ten years ago. I'm not devastated that my marriage is over, and I don't regret one single day of being the wife I was and the mother I am to those two precious children of mine. They are my world."

Devon wiped a tear away from Leanne's cheek.

Leanne sighed, and continued, "I didn't ask for anything in the divorce, except for full custody of the twins. I didn't want the fight, being up against Blake's lawyers. However, they drew the short straw when our case got assigned to a female judge."

Devon whistled and said, "Oh boy."

Leanne smiled and said, "Yup. She gave me full custody and with California being a community state, meaning 50/50 of shared assets; she granted me half of everything. Of course, Blake's lawyer pitched a fit, so I went at them with what I wanted and nothing more. Ten thousand dollars for every one of the ten years I was married to the schmuck, six-hundred-thousand dollars for a house in Seattle, and child support. Blake signed on the dotted line faster than he could say goodbye."

Devon tilted Leanne's head up so that she was eye to eye with him, and asked, "What about visits with the twins? Did they set those arrangements?"

Leanne sighed and said, "Well, the judge told us to work out the visitation schedule with a mandatory four weeks a year to Blake. My lawyer contacted his lawyer's and they told him, and I quote, "Mr. Dougherty is a very busy man. We'll have to get back to you." That's the day I packed our bags, loaded the SUV, and drove to Seattle."

Devon leaned back and said, "Leanne, when exactly was that?"

Leanne looked down. She ran a finger over Devon's chest and said meekly, "July 22nd."

Devon stiffened.

Leanne looked at him and said, "Devon, I needed time. I needed to get my head on right and, most importantly, I needed to spend time with Luke and Lindsey. There wasn't a day that went by that I didn't want to jump on a boat and come to you, but I had to wait. Can you understand?"

Devon leaned his head down against Leanne's and said, "I can. The most important thing is you are here now."

She looked at him and said, "I am."

She kissed him with the tender love that she felt from the top of her head, right down to her tippy toes.

When they finally separated and gathered their wits about them, Leanne said, "I think we should head back now or we'll miss the arrival of the soon to be newlyweds; the ones that should be bare ass naked on this kitchen floor."

They laughed, gathered their clothes which were scattered around the kitchen and got dressed. As they walked down the back stairs hand in hand, Devon pulled Leanne over to the picnic table, lifted her up and sat her on it, then kissed her long and sweet, and said, "I have wanted to kiss you on this table for a very long time."

Leanne smiled wickedly and said, "Oh Romeo, my fantasy on this table with you consisted of a lot more than kissing."

He laughed, kissed her on the nose and they got in the golf cart, and headed back to the big house.

Chapter 36

Leanne and Devon arrived back at the house just as the caterer was setting up a long table on the front lawn. Chet and the kids were sitting on the front porch, watching all the activity. Devon parked the golf cart as Luke and Lindsey came running down the stairs. Excitedly, Luke said, "Mommy, we caught crabs and we put them in a bucket to show you!"

Lindsey, pulling on Leanne's hand, said, "Come on, Mommy. Come see them, I even gave them names!"

Laughing, Leanne said, "Okay, okay, where are they?"

Luke replied, "Down on the dock. Hurry up. Mr. Chet said they can't stay in the bucket too long or they'll die. We wanted to show them to you and then we'll put them back in the water where they live."

Leanne said, "Well, let's go see them."

The three of them ran for the dock.

Devon walked up the stairs to where Chet was sitting and, said, "Looks like crabbing went well."

Chet eyed him and said, "Yup. We had us a good ole time catching them crabs. And from the looks of it, you may have had some fun yourself."

Devon shifted from foot to foot and replied, "Um, well, we set up some lounge chairs on the beach for the newlyweds and dropped the champagne and strawberries off at the cabin."

Chet looked him over and said, "Hmm…that's all, huh?"

Devon cocked an eyebrow at Chet and said, "Well, it took a little longer than expected."

Chet laughed and said, "I bet. You must have been in a rush to get back here, seeing that you got your shirt on inside out."

Devon looked down and said, "Oh bloody hell."

He quickly took off his shirt and turned it right, and put it back on.

Chet laughed a hearty laugh and said, "Good for you, son. You've been waiting for her long enough. Just make sure you do right by her and them two kids."

Devon, looking a little flustered, replied, "I intend to."

Just then, Luke and Lindsey started yelling his name, "Devon, come see the crabs."

Looking across the lawn at the picture in front of him; Leanne and the twins, smiling and laughing; his heart skipped a beat and he was overcome with an emotion he never experienced before. He thought to himself, *this must be what love and happiness feels like.* He took off down the stairs, across the lawn to what he hoped would one day be his family.

* * *

Leanne got the kids bathed and dressed, and told them to go downstairs and watch T.V until she was finished getting ready. She hurried into the shower. She intended to make it quick, since the others would be arriving in an hour.

Twenty minutes later, Leanne was frantically running around her bedroom trying to get dressed. She grabbed the yellow sundress out of the closet and threw it on, slipped on her wedge sandals, and ran into the bathroom. She looked in the mirror and stared at what she saw. She put her hands to her cheeks; she was positively glowing, her face was sun kissed, and her eyes were sparkling like diamonds. She said to herself, "Oh Leanne, you're a goner."

Snapping out of it, she applied her makeup, added a sheer lip gloss, and hurried down stairs to greet the arriving guests.

Leanne walked out onto the front porch and saw Chet, Devon, and the twins holding hands walking across the lawn to the dock where the others had just arrived by boat. Seeing Amber and Leonard get off the boat brought tears to her eyes. She hurried down the stairs, across the lawn towards the controlled chaos on the dock.

Amber was squealing with joy, hugging Chet and Devon. As Leanne approached the end of the dock, Amber caught sight of her and came running at a fast clip straight at Leanne. It only took two seconds to realize they were both going off the edge of the dock and into the water. The others watched in astonishment, until Devon and Chet broke out in laughter. Leonard, who had run to the edge of the dock, looked at the two soaking wet women, and laughed. Everyone headed up the dock toward the beach where Leanne and Amber were struggling to get out of the water. Once on the beach, they collapsed in a fit of laughter.

After a few minutes, having composed themselves, Leonard and Devon walked over to help the women. Trying to un-cling her dress from her body; Leanne, looking at soaking wet Amber, said, "Well, I guess not much has changed." The others being John and Ellen Mathers, Leonard's parents, George and Sylvia Mathers, his grandparents, and the entire Quinn clan were gaping at them.

Amber excitedly said, "Momma, Daddy, this is Leanne."

Leanne, trying to hang on to her dignity in her yellow see-through dress, walked up to them, and said, "Mr. and Mrs. Quinn, it's a pleasure to finally meet you. Amber has told me so much about you. I feel like I have known you for a long time."

Mrs. Quinn walked up to Leanne and wrapped her arms around her, and said, "Same here, and call me Kate."

Amber continued the introductions, "Leanne, these are Leonard's parents, John and Ellen Mathers and his grandparents, George and Sylvia Mathers."

Feeling totally vulnerable in her soaking wet, clinging dress, Leanne walked over to them and shook hands, and said, "It's a pleasure to meet all of you."

They nodded and said likewise.

After all the introductions were finished, the kids and hounds ran up the beach to play on the lawn. Devon put his arm around Leanne as they walked toward the house and said in her ear, "Do you need some help getting out of that wet dress?"

She elbowed him and said, "No thanks, I can manage."

When they reached the house, Leanne grabbed Amber's hand and said, "Come on, Country Bumpkin, let's go get changed."

A half hour later, they came down stairs in shorts and tank tops, foregoing dresses. Leanne and Amber joined the others on the patio, while the kids played in the pool. Everybody was chatting comfortably amongst themselves; cocktails and hors d'oeuvres were being passed around by the catering staff. Devon grabbed two margaritas from the tray and handed one to Leanne.

Amber clinked her glass with a spoon and said, "Y'all, can I have your attention please."

Everyone stopped talking and looked toward Amber, Leanne, Devon, Chet, and Leonard. That's when Amber said, "As you all know, Leonard and I met on this very island, along with Devon, Leanne, and Rosalie. We all came here, somewhat voluntarily, for various reasons, which I have explained to you. We were five, sad, lost, and lonely people, trying to find our way. When we were dropped off on this island, under false pretenses, I might add, we had to survive, and I, for one, know that without these others, I wouldn't have become the person I am today. I am about to marry my Prince Charming and back home with my family that loves me, and, most importantly, finally being true to myself of who I really am. So, for that, I am truly grateful and I want to thank all of you for coming here to Welby Island for mine and Leonard's wedding. Now let's have some fun!"

Everybody raised their glass and said cheers.

Just as Leanne was going to ask Amber where Rosalie was, she heard, "Did I hear someone say let's have some fun?"

All eyes turned to Rosalie walking across the patio, accompanied by a short rotund smiling man in a loud Hawaiian shirt, khaki shorts, and Birkenstock sandals.

Amber squealed and ran straight for Rosalie. Rosalie, seeing her coming, backed up a few paces, but not fast enough. Before she knew it, Amber was on her and the two of them went flying into the pool. The crowd stood there with stunned expressions on their faces. It wasn't until the round man in the Hawaiian shirt let out a bellowing laugh and said, "That must be Amber. Oh, Rosalie is going to be madder than a nest of bees when she gets out of that pool. Took her damn near two hours to get ready; made us miss the boat and all."

Just then, Rosalie and Amber surfaced. Leonard ran over to help them out of the pool. Once up on the patio, Rosalie let loose on Amber, "What the hell, Country Girl! Do you see this dress? It's raw silk; cost me seven hundred dollars and my shoes are on the bottom of the pool, and my hair, oh my God!"

Amber, trying to stifle a giggle, said, "I'm so sorry, Rosalie. I was just so happy to see you. I guess I got a little over excited."

Rosalie, shaking water out of her ear, said, "A little! You took me down in one of your Bailey Jr. tackles; just like you did to Red."

Upon hearing Rosalie, Leanne, Devon, and Leonard bursted out laughing.

Chet brought them some towels and said to Rosalie, "Aww, I've missed you, Firecracker."

He gave her a big hug.

Leanne and Devon walked over and hugged Rosalie. Devon turned to the rotund man, held out his hand, and said, "You have got to be Harold."

Harold boomed, "Yes, indeed. Rosalie has told me about all of you. It's a pleasure to finally meet ya'll in person."

Leanne grabbed Rosalie's hand and said, "Don't be too furious. She took me down into the Puget Sound when she got off the boat. My soaking wet dress is hanging in my bathroom. Let's go get you changed."

They grabbed Amber's hand and the three of them headed into the house, like old times.

Chapter 37

Everyone was gathered at the long table on the front lawn, overlooking the Puget Sound. They were feasting on crayfish, razor clams, mussels, and crabs, along with red potatoes and corn on the cob. Amber was rambling on about how Leanne made this exact same dinner for them at the cabin, and how they spent the day searching for all the shell fish. Leanne was sitting next to Amber's sister, Hannah. Devon was across the table from her, sitting between John and Ellen Mathers.

Hannah leaned toward Leanne and said quietly, "I cannot believe I am sitting across the table from Devon Davis. I have had a crush on him for, like, forever. When Amber told me he was on the island with her, I nearly keeled over. My Heavens, he is such a hunk."

Leanne smiled and said, "He is that."

Hannah said, "So are you going to kiss and tell?"

Leanne pulled back and looked at Hannah and said, "What makes you think we are together?"

Hannah replied, "Oh, it might have something to do with the way he's always looking at you, or the way you're glowing. I may be a country girl, but I can read the language of love better than anyone."

Taken aback, Leanne blushed and said, "Oh, you're good. Amber told me how you handled your momma and daddy when she wanted to go to L.A., so I trust what you're seeing, but I'm still not going to kiss and tell."

They both laughed.

The rest of the evening was filled with laughter and storytelling. As the sun faded into the Puget Sound, the children started to fade, too. Leanne, Hannah, and Jenna gathered the sleepy kids and headed off to put them to bed. Leanne skipped Luke and Lindsey's nightly bath and tucked them into bed, dirty feet and all. As she was sitting on the edge of the bed finishing up the book she was reading to the twins, Devon silently slipped into the room. After she finished the book, she tucked the covers up to the twin's chins, kissed their foreheads and turned to leave, and was startled by Devon standing in the doorway. She quietly said to him, "They are just about out."

Devon touched Leanne's cheek, and asked, "Would you mind if I said good night to them?"

Leanne reached for Devon's hand on her cheek, kissed it, and said, "They would like that."

Devon walked over to the sleepy children, bent down, and kissed the top of Lindsey's head. She reached up and wrapped her tiny arms around Devon's neck, and sleepily said, "Night, Devon."

He walked over to Luke and kissed the top of his head. Luke turned and looked up at Devon, and said, "I like you a lot, Devon. I hope Mommy does, too."

Devon tousled Luke's hair and whispered, "I hope so, too."

Leanne turned the light off and closed the door behind them. She turned to Devon and said, "Oh, Mommy so does like you."

Devon tapped her nose and said, "Good thing, because I'm over the moon about Mommy."

They headed back downstairs to join the others outside.

The men, being John and George Mathers, Lee Quinn, Bailey Jr., Clay, Chet, Leonard, Harold, and Petey were gathered in a circle; smoking cigars, except for Petey, who was trying to justify to his father why he should be allowed to smoke a cigar, being 18 and all.

Chet called over to Devon and said, "Come on over here, son, and tell this young whipper snapper why he can't smoke a cigar."

Devon laughed and said, "I'm afraid I'm the last person to be telling an 18-year-old boy what he can and cannot do."

He joined the group and lit up the cigar Harold handed him.

Petey turned to Devon and said, "They won't even let me have a beer."

Devon put his hands in the air and said, "Mate, if your momma is anything like your sister Amber, I am not crossing her, or I'll end up cleaning the chicken coop for a month."

Amber's daddy, Lee Quinn, laughed, and said to Devon, "You got yourself a good dose of my baby girl, didn't ya, son."

Devon looked over at Amber, Leanne, and Rosalie, smiled and said, "And then some."

Amber looked at Leanne and Rosalie and said, "Let's grab some sweatshirts and head down to the beach. I could sure use some girl time with you two."

All three ran inside and up the stairs to get their sweatshirts. Leanne went to the linen closet, grabbed a blanket, and they headed back down stairs. Rosalie told them to wait for her on the porch, she would be right out.

Amber told her momma and both Mather women, who were sitting in the rockers on the front porch, that she, Leanne, and Rosalie were heading down to the beach for a bit.

Rosalie joined them and the three of them walked down the stairs and across the lawn to the beach. Leanne spread the blanket out and they all sat. Rosalie reached under her sweatshirt and produced a bottle of champagne and three plastic cups. She popped the cork and poured them each a glass.

Amber squealed, "I can't believe we're all together again. I have missed ya'll so much, even though we've talked on the phone. It just wasn't the same."

Rosalie tapped her glass to the others and said, "I can't believe it's been three months. And here, we are back on this island to celebrate your wedding day."

Leanne said to Rosalie, "Now that you mention three months flying by, when exactly did you and Harold reunite?"

Rosalie took a sip of her champagne and said, "Well, the day I arrived home from Seattle I called him and asked him to pick me up, since he had to go get my car the day we left that so called airport. Anyway, I guess he noticed a change in me and asked me to have dinner with him that night at his place. We spent the whole night talking until the early hours of the morning. And, you are going to love this part. Remember how I told you about the day I hit rock bottom that landed me on the road to enlightenment. Harold had come over and I asked him, ever so sweetly, to refill my pain pills and when he said no, I went bat-shit crazy on him. Well, it turns out, all those months he was bringing me pills he was filling the bottle with vitamins. That is what he was going to tell me that day, but I never gave him a chance. Go figure, I wasn't hooked on pain pills after all."

Leanne stunned, said, "Holy crap."

Amber asked, "Why did he let you believe that they were pain pills all that time?"

Rosalie scoffed and said, "Have you met me? He knows I would have gone to someone else to get the real thing, so he figured he would just keep giving me the vitamins. No harm."

Amber smiled and said, "That's a good man, Rosalie."

Rosalie continued her story, "Anyway, he drove me home at three a.m. The next day, when I got to my office, there were a dozen long stem roses waiting for me. I was touched and told him so. From that day on, I received a dozen long stem roses from him, in all these amazing different colors. Finally, after three weeks, I told him it had to stop. My office was turning in to flower shop. So, the next day I'm sitting in my office and I get this delivery. When I open it, there is a huge box of Belgium chocolates. The next day, I come into my office to find a dozen supersized Hershey Kisses all over my desk. This continued for two weeks. Now, I needed to put a stop to the candy invasion, so I marched over to his office and told him, "Harold, you have got to stop with the candy, just like the flowers," and he said, "Well, Rosalie, if you can't decipher my message, then I guess there is nothing left for me to do," and I said annoyingly, "What message are you trying to send with flowers and chocolate…?" And then, it hits me like cupid's arrow to the heart: Sweet Rosalie. During our very brief dating days, before we got married, and every day thereafter, Harold did not let one day go by without calling me, and asking, "How is my Sweet Rosalie this fine day?"

Amber, totally engrossed in Rosalie's story, said, "Aww…that is so sweet."

Rosalie sighed and said, "I realized that day that I missed being his Sweet Rosalie and that I missed him."

Leanne took Rosalie's hand and said, "When you talked about Harold that night at the cabin, I truly sensed that you missed him, and that you might still be in love with him. You deserve to be happy."

Rosalie smiled at her and said, "Well, I guess, I needed to find that out on my own. Right now, we are only officially dating. I told Harold since he swept me off my feet after one month the first time around, this time I wanted to be courted. I want a long courtship filled with fun and adventure. So that is why when we leave the island, we are off on a 14 day Alaskan cruise."

Amber, being Amber, said, "Oooh, I have an idea. Why don't you let Chet marry you and Harold tomorrow, too? Your Alaskan cruise can be your honeymoon."

Rosalie laughed and said, "Nope, Country Girl. Tomorrow is all about you and Leonard. Talking of honeymoons, where are you two love birds heading?"

Amber smiled slyly and said, "Well, after we say our I Do's and celebrate with ya'll, we are heading over to the cabin for a night or two."

Rosalie stopped mid sip and said, "You have got to be kidding me!"

Leanne laughed and said, "Nope, she's not. Devon and I went over there this morning to drop off a special package for you, which is in the refrigerator, and also brought over a couple of lounge chairs and set them up on the beach."

Amber squealed and said, "Really! You two are the best." She hugged Leanne.

Rosalie, still quick on her toes, said to Leanne, "Speaking of you two, being you and Devon, my radar has been picking up signals all night. And it is detecting romance."

Leanne picked up her cup, took a sip and said, "I'm not sure what you're talking about Rosalie."

Rosalie scoffed and said, "Spill it, Locomotive. It is written all over your blushing face."

Amber, just catching on, said, "Oh my God, Leanne. Are you and Devon a couple?"

Leanne, ready to burst at the seams, took a deep breath and said, "Um, well, I moved to Seattle…"

She barely got the words out before Rosalie and Amber both screamed, "What!"

Leanne quickly looked behind her at the others up on the lawn. She turned to the two screeching hens and said, "Hush! I'm not going to tell you one more detail, unless you promise not to scream."

Both hens nodded.

Leanne took another deep breath, and continued, "Well, you both know about what happened with Blake. So, when my lawyer called his lawyers to discuss a visitation schedule, asshole's lawyers told my lawyer, and I quote, "Mr. Dougherty is a very busy man, we'll have to get back to you." That's when I packed up my stuff, the twins, loaded the SUV, and drove straight to Seattle. I bought a small house a few blocks from the marina."

Stunned, Rosalie asked, "When was this?"

Leanne quietly said, "July 22nd."

Amber squealed and said, "You've been with Devon since July?"

Leanne quickly said, "No, no. I never contacted him when I arrived. We agreed to wait until your wedding to see what happened when I went home. Either I show up with my happy family, including Blake, or I show up with just the twins. We weren't due to come to the island until today with the rest of you, but I took a chance and called Chet, who came and got us Thursday. Devon was shocked when the three of us stepped off the boat, but he has taken to the twins from the minute they met. Both he and Chet have been amazing with the kids and they are just so happy."

Rosalie asked Leanne, "But why didn't you tell me when I called to go dress shopping?"

Leanne sighed and said, "I didn't want to tell anyone. I needed time alone with the kids, and time for me to come to terms with what happened with Blake, and also figure out what to do about Devon. Can you understand? I'm so sorry. I didn't want to keep secrets from either of you, but I was afraid one of you would have called Chet or Devon and told them I was only a short boat ride away."

Amber said, "Well, you made a good call on that one, Leanne, because I would have been on that phone faster than a flea on a cat, telling Devon to go find you."

Leanne smiled and said, "Thank you."

Rosalie poured a little more champagne in each of their cups, looked at Leanne and said, "Okay, all is forgiven. Now get to the good stuff, and do not leave out even the smallest of details."

Amber scooted closer.

Leanne took a sip of her champagne, and began, "Okay, I really need to tell you two or I am going to explode. So, we have been tip toeing around each other since I got here. We had a close encounter in the kitchen last night, but the kids and hounds came running in. Anyway, we made plans to ride over to the cabin in the morning to drop off the stuff. When we came out of the woods on the golf cart, I was overcome with seeing the cabin after all these months. I got a little emotional, but pulled it together and we went inside. Devon was putting the stuff in the refrigerator and when he shut the door, I um, well…"

Leanne hid her face in her hands.

Wide eyed, Rosalie said, "Are you telling me that you and Devon had sex in the cabin kitchen?"

Leanne, with her face still in her hands, nodded.

Amber screamed, "Oh my God, Leanne. That is awesome!"

Leanne quickly said, "Hush!"

Digesting this news, Rosalie finally said, "Good for you, Locomotive. Everything I have seen tonight said that that man is totally smitten with you. And as you said to me, you deserve to be happy."

"Thank you," Leanne said to Rosalie, then turned to Amber and said, "I'm sorry we christened the kitchen floor before you and Leonard."

Amber laughed and said, "Well, once we get the hang of the, you know what, there won't be anywhere, inside or out, of that cabin we won't christen."

That sent the hens into a cackling fit of laughter.

Rosalie yawned and said to Amber, "Okay, then. Let's head up to the house. You have a big day tomorrow and apparently an even bigger night ahead of you."

The three rose, picked up the champagne bottle, cups and blanket, and headed across the lawn.

Chapter 38

Leanne woke up to a second consecutive morning of silence. Remembering that yesterday morning the twins chose to wake Devon instead of her, got her up, and moving. She went into the bathroom, washed her face, brushed her teeth, quickly put on a pair of sweat pants and a tank top, then hurried down the hall to Devon's room. She listened at the door, but heard nothing. So, she quietly opened the door and peeked in; relieved to find Devon fast asleep with a pillow over his head. Feeling playful, she tip toed into the room, creeped quietly over to the side of the bed, and reached out to tickle Devon. But, apparently, he was not as soundly asleep as she assumed. With lightning speed, he grabbed both her arms and pulled her onto the bed. When she squealed, Devon laughed and said, "I thought maybe the little tickle terrors were back for more fun."

Leanne laughed and said, "That's what I thought, too, when I woke up to the sound of nothing. So, I decided to come rescue you."

Devon pulled her closer until they were snuggled together and said, "Were you now? It seemed to me you were sneaking in here for a little fun yourself."

Leanne squirmed to get free from his arms wrapped around her and said, "Oh no, Romeo. There is no time for that. If the kids aren't in here tormenting you, that can only mean they are downstairs running circles around Chet."

Devon said, "Well, good then, that gives us a few minutes to ourselves."

Before Leanne could respond, Devon crushed his mouth to hers. Having lost all of her self-control, Leanne responded to his kiss with every ounce of her longing for him.

Devon gently tucked a wild strand of hair behind Leanne's ear, smiled down at her and said, "I missed you."

Leanne touched his lips and replied, "I missed you, too."

Devon kissed her gently and said, "Okay, let's go see what the little ones are up to."

It took Leanne a few minutes to pull herself together after she left Devon's room. She brushed her hair, threw on a sweat shirt and her sneakers, and headed downstairs to the kitchen.

When she walked through the door, she was greeted by the sight of Kate at the stove, Hannah, setting the table, and Amber holding baby Claire, cooing and laughing. She cleared the lump from her throat and said, "Good morning," cheerfully to the other women. Kate stopped what she was doing and walked over to the coffee pot, poured a cup, and handed it to Leanne, adding a kiss on her cheek.

Hannah, looking up and with a sly smile, said, "Well, don't you look like a ray of sunshine. Glowing, actually."

Amber stood up with Claire on her hip and said brightly, "Morning, Leanne. The kids are out front with Chet, looking for crabs."

Leanne, being taken in by the other three women's eyes, said, "Sorry, I didn't get down here sooner. I got, um, a little side tracked."

Hannah laughed and said, "I bet."

Amber, always a few seconds late to catch on, said, "Oh…oh, no worries Leanne. Momma is cooking up a good ole country breakfast and the men folk haven't even surfaced yet."

Kate laughed and said, "We'll, that's because the men folk haven't smelled the bacon yet."

Just as Kate finished her sentence, Leonard walked into the kitchen and stopped dead in his tracks at the sight of Amber with a baby on her hip. He turned a few shades paler as Kate handed him a cup of coffee.

Hannah, never missing a beat, said to Leonard, "Good morning, my soon to be brother in law. You better get used to this sight. We Quinn women pop baby's out like chicken eggs."

Leanne, seeing Leonard wobble a bit, guided him to a chair next to Amber, who in turn placed baby Claire in his lap. All three women watched in amusement as horror crept across his face.

Devon walked into the kitchen in a pair of cargo shorts and no shirt.

Hannah gasped.

Leanne laughed and said to Hannah, "Right?"

Hannah just stared.

Kate handed Devon a cup of coffee, then turned to Hannah, and said, "Go gather everyone for breakfast."

Hannah, wide eyed and jaw dropped, moved towards the door that Devon was partially blocking. He smiled down at her and in his thick British accent, said, "Good morning, Hannah. Did you sleep well in the guest wing?"

Hannah looked up at him and nodded, then took off down the hallway.

Amber giggled and said to Devon, "She had a major crush on you before she met Clay. I think that's the first time I've ever seen her speechless."

Then Kate added, "Rendering her speechless is hard to do. So, thank you, Devon."

The women laughed.

Devon walked over to Leanne and kissed her head, and said, "I'll go put a shirt on."

He left the kitchen.

* * *

After a huge breakfast of eggs, potatoes, bacon, country ham, along with biscuits and gravy, Leanne and Rosalie scooted everyone out of the kitchen so they could clean up.

Kate protested, but Devon put his arm around her and said, "Kate, we had a chore list at the cabin; Leanne cooked and I cleaned. So, why don't you go get off your feet for a bit and spend some time with your soon to be wed baby girl?"

Kate smiled up at him, kissed his cheek, and left the kitchen.

Leanne, Rosalie, and Devon finished cleaning the kitchen just as the caterer's arrived to start preparations for the wedding.

Chapter 39

Leanne, Rosalie, Kate, Hannah, and Jenna sat on the bed in Amber's room. Amber emerged from the bathroom and said, "Okay, girls. Let's do this."

Everyone kicked into gear. Rosalie worked on fingers and toes; giving Amber a mani and pedi. Kate and Hannah got the dress out of the closet and hung it in the bathroom to steam. Jenna, being the owner of her own hair salon, went to work on Amber's hair, and Leanne assembled the old, the new, and the blue on the dresser; along with the tear drop pearl earrings she secretly bought for Amber. Once Amber applied her make-up, it was time to slip into the strapless, Olaff Cassano tea length dress that was a wedding present from Giovanni. It arrived on the Quinn's doorstep a few weeks after Amber arrived home, and was accompanied by a note that read, "*Oh, my sweet Bella. My heart soars with the news of your impending marriage to Signor Leonard. It saddens me deeply not to be able to be there on your wedding day, due to me being in Italy tending to my ailing mother. Please accept this dress as my wedding gift. I pleaded with you many a time to photograph you in it; however, your superstition of bad luck to wear such a dress before you found, as you say, your Prince Charming, kept me from doing so. But now, my Bella, you have found Prince Charming, and I would be honored if you would wear this dress on your special day. And, please, my Bella, send me a photograph of you in it so I can see my vision come to life. Congratulations to you and Signor Leonard. He is a very lucky man. Amore, Giovanni.*"

Amber slid on the dress, as tears slid down her cheeks, remembering the countless times Giovanni begged her to put the dress on; not just because he was a photographer, but because she had turned down an incredible opportunity from

Olaff Cassano himself, who was determined to have Amber be the model for the dress at the famous Italian Fashion Week. Amber never regretted turning down that opportunity, and now, as she slipped into the gorgeous dress, she knew why. This moment was as magical as any bride could wish for. The other five women in the room were rendered speechless; eyes glistening with tears as they took in the beauty of Amber in her wedding dress. Rosalie grabbed a box of tissues off the night stand, wiped the tears from her face, and said, "Okay, enough of this, Amber. You are going to ruin your makeup. And there is no way I am going to stand by your side, in all of your beauty, with a red nose and puffy eyes. Now, let's get you finished so I can try to pull my shit together."

That sent the room into a fit of laughter. Everyone grabbed a tissue, composed themselves, and returned to the task at hand.

* * *

An hour later, at precisely three o'clock in the afternoon; the exact time the five strangers arrived on Welby island three months ago, Amber, on her father's arm, walked down the front porch stairs toward the flower adorned garden arbor where Leonard, her soon to be husband, stood. Devon and Chet were at his side, as were Rosalie and Leanne. The rest of the families turned in their chairs and stared in awe at the sight of Amber in her beautiful dress and wreath of pale pink baby roses in her hair. Leonard stood star struck at the beauty of Amber, his soon to be wife. Devon put his arm around Leonard's shoulder and said quietly, "Looks like you've hit the jackpot, mate."

When Amber reached Leonard, Lee Quinn, with glassy eyes, kissed his baby girls cheek, shook Leonard's hand, and turned to go sit next to Kate.

Chet cleared his throat of the pride and love he was feeling for Country Girl and Leonard and said, "Okay, folks, let's do this."

* * *

The ceremony was short and sweet. Amber and Leonard both expressed their love and devotion to one another in their own words and when Chet pronounced them man and wife, everyone cheered and clapped, then Petey gave a loud whistle and the crowd erupted into laughter.

They ate and danced for hours and when the sun began to set, Devon passed out glasses of champagne and everyone lined up on the beach to toast the setting sun and the newlyweds. They made their way down the beach in the golf cart, which all the kids decorated with trailing red solo cups.

At midnight, when the last of the guests retreated to their rooms, Devon approached Leanne, took her hand, and led her down to the beach. They sat in the sand and stared out at the moon lit Puget Sound in silence. Devon wrapped his arm around Leanne, so she scooted closer, and laid her head on his shoulder. After a few minutes, Devon said, "Can you stay on for a bit after everyone leaves in the morning?"

Leanne sighed and replied, "The twins start school on Tuesday. So, I really should head home and get them ready."

Devon nodded and said, "How about you stay until Monday? Then, we'll all go back to the mainland. Chet has his guy's night out with the geezers. And if you don't mind, I'll stay the night with the three of you and see the kids off to their first day of school."

Leanne slowly turned and looked into Devon's eyes, "They would like that. I would like that."

Devon leaned down and gently kissed her lips, then said, "I have to go out on tour starting October 25th, but we should be wrapped up by the middle of December. Plus, I'll be back and forth in between as often as I can, but I would like to do a little planning ahead, if you are game."

Leanne lifted her head off Devon's shoulder and said, "Such as?"

Devon smiled and tapped her nose, and replied, "Such as, why don't we plan on spending Christmas here on Welby Island? Just us, the twins, and Chet, in a family sort of way. Not that I have much experience with that, but I envision a grand Christmas tree being decorated by the lot of us. A crackling fire, mistletoe, of course, hot cocoa for the kiddies, hot totties for the grownups, a gazillion presents under the tree."

Leanne stood, held out her hand to Devon, and helped him up. When he was standing in front of her, she reached up and kissed him passionately, and said, "I love your vision of Christmas on Welby Island...and I love you."

Together, hand in hand, they headed up the beach and across the lawn to the big house.

The End